The story of a country pastor who
becomes a fighter pilot

TO FLY, TO
FIGHT
and to Save

RICHARD BEMAND

The story of a country pastor who
becomes a fighter pilot

TO FLY, TO
FIGHT
and to Save

RICHARD BEMAND

MEREO
Cirencester

Mereo Books

1A The Wool Market Dyer Street Cirencester Gloucestershire GL7 2PR
An imprint of Memoirs Publishing www.mereobooks.com

To fly, to fight and to save: 978-1-86151-768-5

First published in Great Britain in 2017
by Mereo Books, an imprint of Memoirs Publishing

The address for Memoirs Publishing Group Limited can be found at
www.memoirspublishing.com

The Memoirs Publishing Group Ltd Reg. No. 7834348

Cover Design - Ray Lipscombe

The Memoirs Publishing Group supports both The Forest Stewardship Council®
(FSC®) and the PEFC® leading international forest-certification organisations. Our
books carrying both the FSC label and the PEFC® and are printed on FSC®-certified
paper. FSC® is the only forest-certification scheme supported by the leading
environmental organisations including Greenpeace. Our paper procurement policy
can be found at www.memoirspublishing.com/environment

Typeset in 10/17pt Century Schoolbook
by Wiltshire Associates Publisher Services Ltd. Printed and bound in Great Britain
by Printondemand-Worldwide, Peterborough PE2 6XD

Dedicated to my father, RAF Sergeant
Robert Eric Bemand, who served in Malta during WW2.

Introduction

John Wilkins is a young man who has been taught to fly by his ex-Royal Flying Corps father. He longs to fly in battle, but his Christian beliefs bring him into a pastoral role. When conflict looms again in the shape of World War II, he has to make a hard decision. Should he continue to shepherd the flock in his village church, or should he apply for a pilot's job in RAF Fighter Command, where the need for experienced pilots is growing? This is an absorbing story about a fictional character set in a factual historical setting.

CHAPTER 1

My name is John Wilkins. I was born in our family cottage near a small area of land in the Midlands where my parents Charles and Maria raised a small herd of beef cattle. My parents were married in 1910, and lived there until I was born in 1913, just before the Great War. It was called the War to End All Wars, something which we now know to be wrong, but at the time we were all hoping that a new life of peace would lie ahead of us.

My father Charles had joined the Royal Flying Corps in 1915, at a time when powered flight was still in its infancy, but the excitement of flying through the air was shared by many young men at the time. Ladies' heads turned admiringly towards the young aviators as they strode down the streets in their spotless new uniforms. Unfortunately, for many of those young men, the excitement soon turned to terror.

Even though these early aircraft were made from nothing more than paper and wood held together with tight wires or ropes, they were found to be of immense value during the war. They were used initially for observation purposes, their pilots communicating with the ground in order to direct artillery fire, or for reconnaissance. Most of the early planes had little or no weaponry, so this was dangerous work. As suitable air armament became available planes were developed for offensive purposes, where patrols would go out at set times to attack enemy targets. Because the enemy responded in a similar way the result often ended up in what became known as a dogfight, where aircraft from each side would attack each other and dive, climb or turn either to escape or to attack.

My father spoke of the unlucky ones whose planes were hit either by bullets from enemy aircraft or anti-aircraft fire from the ground, which exploded around them in big black puffs of smoke. In the early days, no pilots were given parachutes on the basis that their weight might make planes too heavy, so the pilots of any aircraft that were hit had no choice but to try and regain control. Very often pilots in damaged aircraft could do nothing but watch in vain as the ground rushed up to meet them, hoping they would survive the crash.

War planes developed very quickly through the years of the conflict. Engines became more powerful and fuselages more streamlined, while armaments changed from simple and ineffective pistols, fired more in hope than expectation of a hit, to sequenced machine-guns that would automatically fire between the propeller blades.

In 1916 new recruits were being told that their life expectancy in a plane whilst at the front was about two weeks, so morale wasn't exactly high. They had all been told "Beware of the Hun in the sun" because the enemy would try to approach them from the direction of the sun to avoid being seen.

In April of that year my father had been flying on patrol in one of the popular Sopwith Pup fighters, which were armed with one belt-loaded Vickers machine-gun on the cowling behind the propeller. He always hinted that in hindsight he would have preferred a highly-manoeuvrable SE5a aircraft, which also had one drum-loaded Lewis gun on the top wing above the pilot, which it was the pilot's responsibility to reload if it ran out of ammunition. However, the SE5a, considered to be one of the best fighters of the war, was not in general supply until the end of 1916.

On one occasion I think my father slightly exaggerated when he claimed that with an SE5a he might have given the top enemy ace, Manfred von Richthofen, "a real spanking"! His patrol of three aircraft was suddenly attacked out of the sun by a squadron of German Albatros D3 planes, which were armed with two forward-firing machine-guns. The planes were painted bright red, and Charles knew that there was only one squadron with those colours, and it meant danger. The aircraft dived upon them, accelerating all the time. One of the Pups went down right away, and I was told that the pilot appeared to be praying. His plane, trailing smoke and still full of fuel, hit the ground with a mighty explosion. My father's plane was also hit and started trailing smoke, whilst he was wounded by several machine gun bullets in his side and lower leg, one of which cracked his shin bone.

Our pilots had been told not to follow a stricken plane down, and I think the enemy must have been told the same, because the Albatros disengaged. Even so, the enemy pilot brought his plane alongside for a few moments and saluted Charles. He always said that had it not been for that piece of chivalry, he might never have survived. He managed to regain control at about 1000 feet and was able to crash-land at one of the nearby emergency airfields on the British side of the lines.

Having been dragged from the wreckage of his plane, he was sent home to England on one of the white-painted hospital ships. On the way down in his crippled aircraft my father remembered seeing the other pilot praying, and suddenly uttered the words, "God, if you really are there, then bring me down safely and I will believe in you for ever!" He was not one to break his promises and so, once life had returned to some sort of normality, my parents joined the local church, where I was christened when I was six years old.

My mother Maria was a very capable nurse who joined the Red Cross in 1915. She was also an attractive girl whose fair hair and blue eyes caught the eyes of many a wounded serviceman. She knew the names of all the patients in the hospital where she worked, some of whom had suffered very severe injuries, and it was often through her care that they recovered. Maria was well known to all the patients, but she and my father always fulfilled their special connection. Maria was allowed to care for Charles, who had been very graciously invalided out of the service, until his full recovery some nine months later, when his injuries forced him to be given other duties, which included the supply of new aircraft to the front.

After the war the Royal Air Force, as the old Royal Flying Corps was renamed, considered many of its aircraft either too old or unnecessary for defence purposes. Being an old pilot, my father had the urge to purchase one, because, whatever else happened, he still wanted to live a life in the air. He managed to contact the few pilots with whom he had flown, and with their help he tracked down his former Commander to see if he could ask a favour, claiming that an aircraft would help him survey the cattle on his land. For this reason he was offered an old RE8, a two-seater biplane, originally used for reconnaissance purposes but now obsolete and no longer required. He already knew that the RE8 had a habit of going into a spin if the pilot accidentally stalled the aircraft, so it would need to be flown carefully.

Because of its age, and some small areas of damage on the wings and fuselage, I think the air force just wanted it out of the way, so my father bought it for almost nothing. Using his skills, together with some help from friends and old comrades, he spent long hours restoring the old RE8 to its original condition, and it soon became his pride and joy. In the early 1920s his task was complete, and one sunny day in May he took the aircraft up for its first flight since the Great War. Even I, as a young boy, could sense the atmosphere of excitement around the cottage as he donned his thick leather flying suit with a warm fur lining, together with his lined boots, helmet and goggles. He said it was like turning the clock back.

As a youth I was eager to follow in my father's footsteps, as some boys do. As my father took the old aircraft up regularly over the next few years I felt that I wanted to be a pilot too, and this was something he actually encouraged by taking me up in the RE8. Once we were back on the ground and the plane was back in the hangar that he had built near to our cottage, he would show me the controls and how to use them. Even in the hangar it was thrilling to sit in the pilot's seat and use one's imagination to enter the surrounding clouds in the sky.

One day he told me to wrap up warm ready for a flight, but when I was about to climb into the observer's seat at the back he told me to wait for a moment. He then climbed into the cockpit and told me to take a seat on his lap. I was still quite small, so I could just about do this. He said it was time for me to try the plane out for myself, and he would manage the take-off with me watching. We would then level off at a reasonable altitude, and I would be given control of the aircraft. He reminded me of all he had taught me, and was confident enough for me to take the stick for the first time ever to give me a sense of what real flying was like. After a short distance flying straight and level he would then take the controls again and take the plane in to land. Everything went well, and as time passed, even though I was still only a schoolboy, my father taught me everything he knew about flying. He was sure that when I came of age I would have no trouble qualifying as a pilot.

In the church too I had followed in my father's footsteps. He had become a sincere and active Christian believer, and we both learned more and more from the Scriptures, which we read regularly. We were like a family with a mission, but as I grew up we were sure there was more to that mission than met the eye. One day the Pastor at our church shared his thoughts with us. He told us God had spoken to him and said we needed some clarity in our lives, which was exactly right. He told us the story of the apostles in the Bible, who considered themselves inadequately prepared, yet to whom Jesus gave the command to "Go ye into all the world and preach the gospel to every creature" (Mark 16:15). They had all believed in Jesus, and they put their faith in Him in order that He might guide their path. In the church were a retired army officer by the name of Edward Jackson, who had formerly been a teacher, and his wife Alice. They opened a small class in our village in order that all the children who came would have the opportunity of a good education, something which everyone thought necessary in the post-war period.

One of the other children in the class was Edward's daughter Ruth, who was the same age as me. As time went by we moved on from just being classmates to a point where we were special friends. Ruth and I went through the classes together, then outside school hours we began to share our duties and our leisure activities. Though Edward could see that we were already beginning to tie a knot between ourselves for the future, he merely smiled and watched us discreetly. I'm sure he guessed that we were beginning to plan for the future, and it was nice to have his approval.

CHAPTER 2

I had always believed in Jesus Christ as my Saviour so, even though I felt a desire to move on and take the first big opportunity that came along after I left school, I sought real guidance from Him. I was still living and working on our farm, but each day I continued to ask God to reveal the right way to me. It was only when the church Pastor approached me one day with an unusual and unexpected question that something just clicked. He asked me quite simply "How would you like to be a pastor?"

My father had apparently told him of my desire to move on, and he believed I had the leadership qualities and the potential to achieve this goal. The Pastor added that he was getting older, and the need for an obedient young man to take over the Pastorate at a later, if as yet unknown date, was becoming ever more apparent. Because this was only a small church in a small village with a small population, no elders had ever been chosen, yet he believed that having a deputy pastor to take on the mantle where necessary would be an ideal way of pressing on. However, he warned that it would be a hard task, saying that to preach on 48 Sundays in the year, as well as to take control of other internal duties such as Sunday School, marriages and funerals, together with any counselling or visits that might be requested, would be no picnic, and the course itself could last for about three years, assuming that my studies went well.

I felt at first as if I were a David rising up to face Goliath (1 Samuel 17). How could I possibly endure and complete such a mighty task? I also felt that this might change my life for ever, and I wasn't sure about that to start with. Would I end up as an unmarried hermit living in a church rectory? But I remembered that David had actually beaten Goliath armed with nothing but a sling, something which eased my mind a little, so I decided to consider what the Pastor had said. Though I was sure I didn't want to be honoured in quite the same way, I remembered that the people even made David their King (2 Samuel 5).

The first people I spoke to about the Pastor's proposition were my parents. It soon became clear that he had spoken to them earlier, and they guessed quite rightly that the initial atmosphere would be one of uncertainty. With great understanding they reassured me and said that my father

Charles had always wanted to do something similar, and he would be proud if I, as his son, could in effect take on his mantle and achieve this task for both of us. I then spoke to my Ruth, as I now saw her, with her mother and father in the background. I told her of my fears, and also of the fact that our friendship might suddenly be split apart if I were to make the wrong decision. When Edward stepped forward to address me I wasn't sure what to expect. I didn't even know if he might turn me out of his house for not wanting to continue my special friendship with Ruth. Yet in his response Edward also mentioned that he, as an army officer, had been privileged to have contact with some of the army chaplains he had met during the Great War, and he said that he too would be proud to see me as a pastor. One of those same chaplains had given him a special Bible text to remember, that said "Trust in the Lord with all thine heart and lean not onto thine own understanding; in all thy ways acknowledge him, and he shall direct thy paths." (Proverbs 3:5-6)

Even Ruth was in tears, but they were tears of joy, not sadness. She gently put her arms around me and expressed her love for me, stating that she would always write and if I had to go away to train, she would be there waiting for me when I returned. It was as if our long, close friendship had suddenly blossomed into something new.

When I returned home the Pastor was waiting for me, and I commented that his offer was a big opportunity, but I would need to pray about it personally before I made any final decision. In my prayers that night, and for the rest of the week, I told God how strange I would feel if I had to leave my home, my parents, my friends and the rural environment which I had come to feel a part of. I also prayed about my feelings for Ruth in particular, asking him to direct my path and open the right doors. I would soon be reaching the age when girls were almost looked upon as a should-have, whilst having a family of one's own would be the ultimate desire of a young man like myself.

It wasn't until the following Sunday that the final decision was made. After the regular Sunday service the Pastor drew me aside for a moment. He had spoken to the Bishop in charge of church administration in the area. The Bishop even agreed that it would be a good idea for the Pastor to take on a trainee, and believed that the slightly under-populated rural environment in which the church was set would also help to reduce the stress, and later increase the confidence, of the trainee who had to learn to stand up and be heard in front of all the local population who attended every Sunday. It was agreed that any trainee should attend a suitable course at an approved Bible college for at least 12 months, after which the Pastor himself had agreed to act as my tutor for the rest of the regular three years which the course usually took. Having completed this course, I would attend a suitable examination course. This was quite amazing to me, because it meant I would not be away for as long as I had previously expected, and I would be under our trusted Pastor's wing for much of the time. He told me it would not be easy, but reminded me of his Bible college motto, which emphasised that a man with gifts needs to be trained if he is to use his gifts effectively. It reminded me of the words of St. Paul when he wrote to the church at Corinth, saying "Even so ye, forasmuch as ye are zealous to have spiritual gifts, seek that ye may excel to the edifying of the church." (1 Corinthians 14:12)

The next time I saw Ruth I told her about my plans to take the course, and she was very happy for me. She revealed to me that when her father Edward had gone to fight in the Great War he had taken a small Bible with him, which had been presented to him by the Pastor and members of the church where they had lived. As she grew up, Edward had used his precious Bible to teach her some of the basic Christian messages, and we could possibly share our knowledge of the Bible as I did the course. All the time she would be there to provide mutual support and encouragement. She even mentioned that once the course was complete we would both be in our early twenties, and that would be an ideal time for us to get together, not as mere friends, but as a loving couple.

Over the next few weeks my life was filled with endless thoughts of what lay ahead, together with a host of preparations. I had never been to any form of college before, so my imagination tended to run riot with what I might find there, or what I would need to take with me. Should I take my own pens and ink? Would there be exercise books available? Would I be told which text books to read? It would be the first time I had been away from home for any length of time.

The college to which the Pastor had referred me was the newly-constructed Carlington Bible College, which lay about 30 miles to the west of us. The Principal was a highly-respected gentleman named the Reverend Harold Greenaway. He was one who insisted on hard work, discipline and obedience. It sounded as if he had an army background as well. Later, when I read some of the college booklets, I was proved right, because it mentioned that the former Major Greenaway had been based with one of the main infantry battalions that had taken part in the Battle of the Somme in 1916, where he had gained the Military Medal. I think the Somme changed many people's lives, because on the first day of the battle in July over 50,000 casualties, over 20,000 of which were fatal, were incurred by the British Army, more than at any other time in its history. Just like many of the other soldiers who took part in the Battle of the Somme, because of the tragic circumstances it must have had an enormous impact upon his life, and Harold would never openly talk about the battle.

Meanwhile my father insisted that he would manage whilst I was away. He had had the idea that he could use the old RE8 as a small but reliable air transport service. If others had appointments in areas that were difficult or time consuming to reach, then he would be there to take them if required. As for ferrying goods, he made the observer's seat detachable to make more room. He had laid out a short strip of land in our one field to act as a take-off and landing area, and he knew that aircraft only needed a short area of grass to land in. He would maintain the aircraft himself and act as the ferrying pilot at all times. A friend of his at the local garage had offered to supply fuel, and he also provided a couple of spare petrol cans to take on longer trips. The addition of a new telephone line to the village should also help. My father certainly thought a telephone would be worthwhile, but the bulky old phone we were given was rather unsightly. He wondered if, in the far-distant future, telephones would be shrunk to fit into one's pocket and be carried around. If so, then he wished he were a time-traveller so he could go into the future and bring one back. Some hope!

As term-time gradually drew closer, I felt as if there were some force trying to deter me. It was as if someone was telling me that I did not have the ability to do the course, or endure the strict timetable, and I would be better off leaving it just to help my parents, who were getting older. This was a concern that I shared with the Pastor, but he told me that he was sure that God had led me to do this, although Satan would do his utmost to stop me. He also mentioned the

Lord's Prayer, which contains the words "And lead us not into temptation" (Luke 11:4b), reminding me that each day I needed to pray that the Holy Spirit would lead me and build me up inside. We reel off the Lord's Prayer so much, yet I wonder if it becomes more of a habit than anything. How often do we really consider or think about the words that we know so well? Do we even mean them, or has their repetition just become another church routine?

Early in September 1930, after all my final packing had been done and my goodbyes said, I took the train to Carlington. Once I had reached my destination it was easy to get a lift to the college itself because there were other students travelling with their parents by car. As I entered the gates of what seemed to be an enormous building I just had to look up and thank God for having given me this opportunity.

Having reached the college I was introduced to the Principal himself. To me he was clearly the sort of person who wanted hard work and obedience from all his students, but I was sure that behind that rugged old face of his there was an understanding and kindly heart. Though it was not mentioned, I guessed that he had taken on this job as one means of coming to terms with the huge losses during the battle of the Somme. I also met the course tutor, who would supervise my progress as time went by, and I think he could see that my one ambition was to complete the main course, especially after our Pastor had been to all this trouble and put so much trust in me to do it. I was later given a short tour of the college buildings and shown the dormitory where I would be sleeping with 11 or 12 other students. Having never been to a college before, the corridors and classrooms seemed just like a maze at first, but I was soon reassured that after the first couple of weeks I should find my way around quite easily.

Later that day I met some of my dormitory mates. Most of them were welcoming, but there were a few who wondered how a student from some rural out-of-the-way village could possibly have reached a standard to take part in the pastoral training course. To this I responded that most of the apostles whom Jesus chose were not from middle or upper class families, but were local working men like fishermen. I also reminded them of one of St. Paul's epistles, which contains the text "For ye see your calling, brethren, how that not many wise men after the flesh, not many mighty, not many noble, are exalted. But God hath chosen the foolish things of the world to confound the wise; And base things of the world, and things which are despised, hath God chosen, yea, and things which are not, to bring to nought things that are: That no flesh should glory in his presence." (1 Corinthians 1:26-29) I think some of them were quite surprised to find that I already knew parts of my Bible in such a way but, after this, I became respected and one of the gang, so to speak.

The course itself would be in several parts. These would be:

(a) A study of the Scriptures

Much of it would be to do with a study of the Bible, the background to each book and the messages it contains. We would also be taught particular facts or methods of writing that help identify the author, especially if more than one book is attributed to them.

(b) A study of the languages used in the Bible, like the old Hebrew and Greek texts, and whether later Bible translations had either retained the original meaning, or perhaps applied a similar yet not completely true meaning. This might particularly be found in the words of the Old Testament.

(c) Preaching

This would look at how a Pastor might prepare a particular sermon, which would be a regular task. There were dates in the calendar, such as Easter or Christmas, that might influence the message contained in the sermon, but this could no doubt apply to other external events as well. A part of the curriculum also involves practical experience, and no doubt our Pastor at home would give me a taste of this, whilst offering me some of the hints that he has gained over his many years of experience.

(d) Systematic theology

In this we would consider the Bible's message doctrine by doctrine, rather than book by book. This would help us to provide a message in full, possibly one that might cover related scriptural texts from several books, rather than look at the background to each individual book.

(e) Church history

In this we would be looking back at the early church, how it was founded and how it grew in the early days, then the church as it was during the medieval period. From this we would move to the Reformation period during the 16th century, a time when Protestants began to question some of the Catholic ideas and practices through the church, and the rise of nonconformity. In English church history, the term 'nonconformist' was used to describe a Protestant Christian who did not "conform" to the governance and usages of the established Church of England. Finally we would be studying the evangelical revival, which began during the first part of the 18th century, to the present-day church.

Even in those first few weeks I learned so much in my studies. There were things that I never knew of before, and to be made aware of them through such eloquent tutors made it all stand out so well. There was also the college library, where the numerous shelves held a large selection of books, both old and new, that covered every subject mentioned in the course. There was such a realm of knowledge there just waiting to be rediscovered. I seemed to spend many hours reading and writing, but there always seemed to be something else I found to look at, sometimes a controversial subject, sometimes a simple practical experience that one might find in everyday life.

During some of the time I had free I made sure to send letters to all at home. Not only did I received a letter from the Pastor, offering me his full support with a blessing, but a number of the church members also wrote, and showed their kindness by offering to support me both in their prayers and financially. I would never have expected this, but I think it's a way through which God is demonstrating that this is the way he wants me to follow. I had letters from my parents and, as I was hoping, a special letter from Ruth and her father Edward. Every time I read what she said, I felt sure we were drawing ever closer together. Our love for each other seemed to be growing stronger by the day.

CHAPTER 3

It was now nearly Christmas 1930. At the college we took part in the periodical examinations, and I was certainly pleased with the results. There were some subjects I would have to spend a little extra time studying, because where items covered a range of names, dates and sources, the only way I could take them in properly was to go over the essential points time and time again. I had made some good friends by now, and we all shared our addresses should we wish to contact each other. One of the main problems was one of the students who shared our dormitory. He snored terribly, and some of us reflected that if there were any way to keep us awake at night and distract us from our quiet times, as well as causing us to lose our concentration during our daily lessons because of a lack of sleep, then Satan himself could not have found a better way of doing it.

I was looking forward to taking the train back home for Christmas. My parents, and Ruth most of all, would be glad to see me back safely. They knew that even though my studies had been hard work, I had been able to focus on them and reach a fairly good standard in all the subjects covered during this first term. I would have loved to take them all a Christmas gift, but my time was so taken up with my studies during the week, and the recreational activities at the weekend, that I hadn't been able to go out and get anything. I think they did understand.

Back at home my father was telling me of his exploits in the old RE8. Not everything was easy. One day he was up ferrying some goods to a given destination when the wind suddenly arose and cracked one of the struts holding the biplane's top and bottom wings together. He was forced to land in a grassy field near to which he had seen a road. Once he was able to leave the plane and head for town about a mile away, he found a local carpenter who agreed to repair the wooden wing strut for him. This delayed him for over a day, though he was able to contact Maria by telephone to explain what had happened. The goods too were eventually delivered, though because they were late he had to offer the customer some discount, which was readily accepted. It was amazing that the plane, which was now 15 years old and made of little more than wood and paper, was in such good condition, but I have always said it was his pride and joy.

Being the wintertime, the weather was often cold, and this no doubt affected the number of duties he could perform. I was sure he knew my feelings for Ruth, because he told me he was putting a small amount of cash in a savings box ready for when I might need it in the future.

Ruth and her parents welcomed me into their home when I saw them again on the day after my return from college. There was so much Ruth and I wanted to talk about, much of it concerning the present, but another part of it concerning our future. Being in love with a girl is one thing, but being able to support each other as a family is a totally different subject. We each had our own ideas about our lives together, and we had to look ahead and make our own plans. There were bound to be disagreements about each other's plans, but there had to be a bit of give and take at all times. I did not wish to be hasty, but if we were to marry we had to look at plans for where we might live, what we might do for an income and, at a later date, how we might raise a family.

Later I went to see the Pastor, the man whose trust had enabled me to take a place at college in the first place. I was eager to show him my examination results. He was very pleased for me and said that this was the best way he could have hoped for in which to repay his trust. He also told me of a strange sign that he had received one night, when he awoke in what sounded like a thunderstorm. He lit a candle, only to hear the words "Light is sown for the righteous and gladness for the upright in heart. Rejoice in the Lord, ye righteous; and give thanks at the remembrance of his holiness." (Psalm 97:11-12) When he went out the following morning he mentioned the thunderstorm whilst he was in the local general store, but the grocer there replied that there had been no rain at all. He suddenly understood that God had been speaking to him, and he realised what God had meant by the light and the joy. It was through God's light that everything had come about, and he was receiving the joy in his heart from his act of faith.

The following Thursday was Christmas Day, so we went along to the church for the special Christmas service, conducted by the Pastor. Half-way through the service the Pastor unexpectedly called me up to the front and for the benefit of the congregation, he asked me a few short questions about my life and progress at college. But then came an even more unexpected sequel. He reached up into the pulpit and brought out a beautiful Bible with leather cover and silver trim, which he presented to me on behalf of all the church members. Inside the front page were the names of many church members who had signed it. It was quite a touching thought, and for a moment I was at a loss for words, but in a moment I told them how grateful I was for their gift, and said I would make every effort not to let them down as I continued with the course.

After the service my parents and I were invited to join Edward, Alice and Ruth for a Christmas dinner, which we heartily enjoyed. Alice had been busy for several hours steaming a beautiful goose for the main course, followed by a large Christmas pudding. We all felt very full when we left.

On New Year's Eve Ruth came round to our house in the evening so we could see the New Year in together. As the old tune 'Auld Lang Syne' rang out from the nearby houses, we remembered the old tradition of taking a kiss under the mistletoe, but I think we took the opportunity to make it more than just one. It was the first time we had done anything like that, but it went a little further toward sealing our future. I told her that I would be thinking about her all the time, and added that her letters were special and gave real encouragement in my studies.

On my return to the college for the new term at the beginning of January 1931 I found that there were a few changes. There were students who had just found the work too much for them and had therefore dropped out. Meanwhile it was necessary to make a few adjustments to my timetable because we were told that the different subjects would be covered in rather more depth, which meant that provision was made for anyone who felt they needed help with a particular subject. For instance, before I came to the college I had never heard of anything like systematic theology, and it took time for me to get a thorough understanding of what it represented.

As with any student, I found some of the subjects on the curriculum harder than others. Church History wasn't too bad at all, and each day I would delve into the old history books in the college library to find the information that I wanted. Initially we had to understand the basic facts about the four periods in church history, and history was never one of my better subjects. It was more a case of looking at particular time zones and then expanding on the basic events. It took a good deal of time both reading and writing, but as time went on everything seemed to open up and become that much clearer.

As the cold winter weather gradually gave way to the milder days of spring my time became busier, and likewise as the spring changed to summer. Time seemed to fly by, but when one is so busy that is only to be expected. Yet in June I arrived home feeling quite triumphant, because all my examinations had gone well, though there were times when it was necessary for God to guide my pen a little more than usual. At the time I wasn't sure how much more of the college I would be seeing, simply because of my Pastor's offer to act as my tutor. I had also made some good friends during the course, and I didn't feel it was right just to drop out of the college so suddenly in this way.

However, the Pastor had already invited me to attend a lunch with him on the Sunday, after the service in the church. I was pleased to accept, but I was quite surprised when I arrived on his doorstep at the Rectory to find that he had also invited the area Bishop as well. In a more formal atmosphere I would have been seeking to address the

Bishop as "Your Grace" and, because we had never met previously, I wasn't quite sure what to expect from him. However, when we were introduced to each other by the Pastor I found a mature man who was completely committed to following God's way, but with a good sense of humour as well. He told me that this was a totally informal meeting, and that we could address each other by our first names. He was called Michael, which seemed right because the Archangel Michael in the Scriptures was a warrior and a protector of Israel, and I saw the Bishop as a man with the responsibility of protecting and caring for a flock made up of many tribes.

During our meal he congratulated me on my achievements at the college. One thing I probably didn't know, he said, was that my Pastor had himself been at one time a former tutor at one of the larger bible colleges, hence his reason for allowing him to act as my tutor. Some of the tutors at my college were well-known to him and they had agreed to this unusual plan, but they also suggested that I should keep in close touch with them, and possibly even stay at the college for short periods regularly in order to review or assist my progress. This was a necessity that the Pastor had both considered and recommended, and I too felt that it would benefit me greatly. There was a special atmosphere in such a rural environment where most people knew each other, and since I had grown up in that environment it would be an ideal way of both keeping the current church active but also, wherever possible, to spread God's word to others in the area. He was convinced that church members trusted me not only because I was one of them, but because I had already demonstrated to them that I would honour that trust, which could be seen from my college results.

Later that day I went to see Ruth to tell her the good news. I found her at home and feeling a little sad, because her father had been diagnosed with severe arthritis, an illness for which there was no cure, and which would gradually cripple him. It was seen as a terminal illness. During this time she and her mother would no doubt have to care for a number of his needs. Whilst Ruth and I had grown up and grown closer together, Edward had been a friend as well as a father. I could understand the sadness she felt, but the only thing I could really do at the time was to say that I would remember them all in my prayers.

CHAPTER 4

Before I returned to college in late September 1931 to collect all my clothes and books and to tell the others in the dormitory what had been planned for me, the Pastor took me to one of the church prayer groups for a little practical experience. We started off with a couple of familiar hymns, then the Pastor officially opened the meeting in prayer. About half-way through, just before the time when we looked at and discussed particular Bible texts, he passed control over to me to lead the prayers. I had always attended the groups in the past, so I was confident enough to take charge. There would be prayer requests, to which I added Edward's name, and notices of how those who had been prayed for at previous meetings were managing. I then led all the prayers. There was a period when others would say their own prayers, and I then concluded the prayers and passed control back to the Pastor. I think he was pleased to see that I had the confidence to step out and do this.

Once back at the college, I met the Principal once again. He encouraged me to take a positive attitude toward the course, adding that whilst I was away I could always contact him if I needed any specific help, and that the main course tutors, together with the library, would always be available. We discussed a timetable, and considered how regularly I should return to the college. My Pastor had been given a copy of my curriculum, but the Reverend Greenaway proposed that I should return to the college and stay for one week every two months. This would enable the tutors to effectively check my progress. It also meant that the Pastor would not be under excess pressure if I needed help with relevant subjects.

Everything seemed in order, and the Principal provided me with a prepared timetable to show the regular dates for my return. The timetable had been arranged to include the examination dates in my visits, which meant that I would be able to prepare for them and also sit them with my friends from the college, who had been made aware of my circumstances and were very supportive. They were joking that it would be another two years before they would have the opportunity to join a church, whereas I was lucky to have everything set up for me. I did slip a hint about my personal life as well, but they all wished me well for the future. I asked them to keep in contact whilst I was away, because it was always good to hear from them, and added that I would see them again in seven or eight weeks' time. I also met the tutors who had taught me up to this point, offering them my thanks for the wisdom that they had shared, but they too laughed, and said that they would be pleased to see me when I returned in eight weeks. A couple of the main tutors drove me to the station in order to catch the train back home.

By the time I got back home it seemed as if everything was moving so quickly, yet so smoothly. It was as if God had planned it all in good time. I took a long afternoon's rest on the Monday to get everything sorted in my own mind, then had a good night's sleep to make sure I was ready to take my first lessons from the Pastor the following day. I was still wondering in my own mind what it would be like, but in my prayers that night I just asked God to lead me and prepare me for the next stage of the journey he was taking me on. I remembered the words of the apostle Peter, who wrote that "Ye also, as lively stones, are built up a spiritual house, an holy priesthood, to offer up spiritual sacrifices, acceptable to God by Jesus Christ." (1 Peter 2:4). On the other hand, I guessed that at some time or other I would have to face temptation or trials, and I resolved to face them not on my own, but with the instilled power of the Holy Spirit.

When I came to the rectory early on the Tuesday morning, the Pastor was waiting for me. There was a spare room there which had originally been designed as a small storeroom, but the Pastor had had it adapted for use as an office. That room now became my classroom, and each day I was enlightened by the wisdom of the man whom everyone knew as a simple country Pastor. Often we looked at particular sections of the curriculum for a full morning or a full afternoon, but he would always ensure that I had a full understanding of one section before we moved on to another. There were also studies for me to complete at home, some of which took several hours.

Over the next 18 months the Pastor not only taught me about the subjects given in the college curriculum but went to the point of giving me a fuller understanding of people. He used his imagination to describe those with particular needs, many of which were of a financial, spiritual, or personal nature, and offered me instruction on how I might deal with people with those needs. I found he was a great actor, because during a short break he would on occasion disappear from the room quite suddenly, then suddenly reappear in the guise of a complete stranger who was in need of help. It was an ideal way of training me for the real thing.

Every couple of months I returned to the college for my regular review and progress check, and in some respects they were very pleased with my work. They told me at the end of the second year that my progress had been quite unexpected, because even they had had early suspicions about my being taught outside the college area, but it appeared that everything had worked out.

However, there was one thing I had wanted to do for a long time. In February 1933 I was at the college with my friends, and we were all eagerly looking forward to our final examinations the following July, when I was asked what my plans were for the future. I must have mentioned Ruth, the way she and her parents had supported me throughout, and our feelings for each other. Cecil, who had been appointed as the head of our dormitory, looked at me very calmly and almost influentially, telling me discreetly that for once I should do what my heart was saying. We would both be 21 years old in a few months' time, so it would be right to speak to Ruth not merely about my own future, but about our future together.

When I returned home the following week I called round to see Ruth and her parents. Edward looked up from his chair with a smile when I entered the room, but one could see that he had become weaker since my last visit home. The arthritis from which he suffered had really taken hold, and his hands had become more swollen. It was difficult to know what to say at first, because it was the first time I had seen him in such pain, and with such severe restrictions on his movement. He called Ruth and me forward together and spoke up as we stood before him holding hands. First of all he asked me clearly what my feelings were for Ruth. I replied quite honestly that Ruth and I had grown up together, and that at a later date I would like to be with her for ever. He asked Ruth the same question, what her feelings were for me. She too responded that through our connection and friendship over the years, we had grown not only to understand each other, but to love each other.

There was one other question for me. If and when we did create our own family, would I promise to keep Ruth safe and give her the care and love she wanted? His marriage to Ruth's mother Alice had been long and prosperous because they had each made a sincere commitment to the other, and carried out their family responsibilities to the utmost. I think he had heard all the news about Germany and almost anticipated that there might be another conflict at some time in the future. I told him of one of the passages in the Bible that spoke about marriage, and read the of the apostle Paul's messages about marriage, which said: "Husbands, love your wives, even as Christ also loved the church, and gave himself for it: That he might sanctify and cleanse it with the washing of water by the word. That he might present it to himself a glorious church, not having spot, or wrinkle, or any such thing, but that it should be holy and without blemish. So ought men to love their wives as their own bodies. He that loveth his wife loveth himself. For no man ever yet hated his own flesh, but nourisheth and cherisheth it, even as the Lord the church: For we are members of his body, and of his bones. For this cause shall a man leave his father and mother, and shall be joined unto his wife, and they two shall be one flesh." (Ephesians 5:25-32)

I'm sure that this quite convinced him, because as we stood there before him he lifted up his hand to make the sign of the cross upon us, giving his blessing upon us for the future. It was a really touching moment, one that surprised even Ruth, but we almost knew by that time that we were meant for each other. I paused for a moment, then politely said that there was a question I wanted to ask. He looked puzzled for a moment, and replied with some curiosity that I was quite at liberty to do so. This gave me the opportunity that I had wanted for a long time, so I turned to Ruth, instinctively got down on one knee, and asked her to be my wife. I showed her the ring I had saved up for, and offered it to her. Having glanced quickly at Edward, she looked at me and said "Yes!" It became the happiest moment of my life.

Almost immediately we started planning for the future, but Edward's wisdom showed up once again when he advised "Don't run before you can walk". He stressed that I was at an important stage with my pastoral course, and that I should focus on that until it had been completed. Then we could move to the next stage, which was to find a suitable home for us to create a family. He had his own thoughts about this matter, which weren't revealed to us until after my final examinations the following July.

The Pastor himself drove me to the college late in June for me to revise all my studies before the examinations came. Though my tutor had moved on, the rest expressed their support, not only because they had seen my work in person, but also because of what the Pastor had shared with them. He told them of some of my strengths and weaknesses, but added that overall I had been an excellent student and thoroughly deserved to make the grade. I admitted that the Pastor was an exceptional tutor, but reminded the tutors that I wanted to pass out of my gratitude to him, as well as the promise that I had made to the church members. Before he left, the Pastor and I had about 15 minutes to ourselves in one of the smaller rooms in the college, and together we shared our thoughts and prayed that my examinations would go well.

Being the final examinations, time seemed to pass more slowly before each one. I wanted to get them over and done with, and as one was completed I just longed for the next one to come soon. There was also the project, which needed to be assessed with some care.

However, there came the day when everything was at last done, and all I had to do was to await notification of the results. These took some time to come through, probably because of their importance, but soon after Ruth's birthday on 10th August the Pastor called in to our cottage and announced to my parents "I have your son's results!" I had apparently passed with a commendation.

CHAPTER 5

That Sunday during the church service, the Pastor officially announced my success to the congregation. When he invited me up to the front to say a few words I just had to say that I believed I had honoured the trust that they had put in me at the beginning, and felt that their support right through had demonstrated their belief in me. I added that God had brought me this far, but I would certainly ask Him to direct my path here.

In November 1934 the college held a celebration dinner for all those who had successfully passed their examinations. Later that day an official ceremony took place in the great hall of the college, when the Principal presented certificates and other awards to the successful students. Both my parents were present, together with the Pastor and last, but not least, my wife-to-be, Ruth. Each student climbed the steps to the stage to the applause of the audience, and as the Principal presented our awards he gave each one of us a special Scripture text to remember. To me he said "Commit thy works unto the Lord, and thy thoughts shall be established." (Proverbs 16:3) The Principal had another way of saying it. He always insisted "Whatever you do in faith, do well, and your plans will succeed." To me those few words were almost a revelation of the past, when I had asked the Lord to guide me in this course, yet also a hint of what was to be, not only when I became a major part of our church, but also after Ruth and I were married.

During all this time of celebration, history was being made in another part of Europe. It is said that Satan will do anything to cause strife in the world. In Germany there was elation at the election of a new Chancellor, Adolf Hitler. When he took control of the country it was in a poor economic state, still being forced to repay the debts laid upon it after the Treaty of Versailles was signed at the end of the Great War. The armed forces were also limited in size to ensure that they would not be in a position to start another conflict. However, Hitler soon appeared to have used many means by which to gain control of the country, including fear and manipulation. In July 1934 he demonstrated his anti-religious, and particularly anti-semitic, feelings when his soldiers brought about the destruction of synagogues and other religious buildings. Books written by Jews and others whom Hitler claimed were not part of the new German state were simply brought out onto the streets and burned, even though some of the same books had been used or read in libraries, including university college libraries, for many years. When the aging President (and former Field Marshal) Paul von Hindenburg died on 2nd August, Hitler immediately claimed full control, unscrupulously shaming other government ministers, and openly declaring that such men could not be trusted with the position of President. One of Hitler's main followers, Josef Goebbels, then declared that the post of President was to be merged with that of Chancellor. Hitler, having unscrupulously taken control of the political side of the country, then took over the armed forces, declaring himself to be the Supreme Commander. Yet all the misdeeds that might have occurred seemed to disappear into the minds of many Germans when his charismatic speeches promised to lift Germany out of the gloom into a new era when the country would once again be seen as a great world power, and there were signs that Hitler was already taking measures to reorganize the German economy. The government, now made up almost entirely of his supporters in the National Socialist movement, went along with this completely, and plans were made not only to improve employment and the standard of living but to rebuild the armed forces to a suitable number, all contrary to the Treaty of Versailles. More jobs were created, though the nature of some of them was unclear.

Having been given the text from the book of Proverbs in

the Old Testament, I had decided to refresh my mind on it once again. Some of these early proverbs cover the benefits of wisdom, which is understandable, simply because one of the authors is said to be King Solomon, whom God blessed with the gift of wisdom. Though our path is guided by God's Holy Spirit as we look to Him in prayer, there is much reassurance to be found in texts like Proverbs 3:25-26, which says that we should "Be not afraid of sudden fear, neither of the desolation of the wicked, when it cometh. For the Lord shall be thy confidence and shall keep thy foot from being taken." Now that I was well set in the course, I certainly didn't want to turn away.

Even so, day after day the radio seemed to broadcast more and more news about Hitler and the new Germany he intended to create. He had only been a corporal in the German army during the Great War, so there were those who doubted his ability to command the mighty military force that was already appearing, yet because he had introduced a political side to his life, and convinced many people of his overall ability, there were also those whose reaction was one of both caution and suspicion. The question on many people's lips was whether he wanted to start another war. No one knew.

The Pastor had already told Bishop Michael of my success, and when the Bishop visited the village soon afterwards there appears to have been much conversation about me. The Bishop certainly didn't want the Pastor to step down right away, because he believed that he still had a few years left in him and that his sudden resignation might cause problems. They both agreed, however, to my appointment as a deputy Pastor. It provided a period of transition from a Pastoral life that was indicated in books to one where reality was the question. Being a deputy Pastor had two sides to it. It meant that I would not be automatically inducted, which might have been the case if I had been appointed immediately by the Church of England as a full Pastor. However, even though I would have a responsibility in the church, it also meant that I could have time to myself. It was the Pastor who very much read my thoughts, and was sure that I had skills of a different nature that I might wish to use.

One of these, he was to discover later, was my desire to fly. During my time at college my father had been honing my skills as a pilot. He had many contacts, both veterans of the RFC and other pilots who flew from clubs around the country. A flight instructor from the South West Midlands agreed to take me up in his new Tiger Moth. The De Havilland Tiger Moth DH82A was an open cockpit biplane produced in the 1930s that looked remarkably like one of the old Great War fighters. Its 130-horsepower Gypsy engine gave it a cruising speed of about 80 knots. First of all the instructor took me up in the observer's seat, then told me to make sure I was strapped in tight. He then put the Tiger Moth into a series of aerobatic manoeuvres which were far beyond the straight and level flight I was used to in the old RE8. He told me when we landed back at the airfield that the RAF was now using the Tiger Moth as its primary trainer aircraft, and added that if I ever wanted to join then this was the plane to learn in. I didn't know at the time how much that fact would actually help me at a later date.

Back on the ground he put me in the pilot's seat to show me all the controls and then, quite unexpectedly, asked me if I thought I could do a short flight myself. Unlike the early days of the Great War, when hand signals were the only means of communication between pilots, a radio link had been introduced so that, in the Moth, pilot and observer were in constant contact with each other. This meant he could remind me or instruct me on the controls during the flight.

The next half-hour was quite thrilling for me. As I took off from the grassy strip I realised that for the first time I was in control of a modern plane, one that was recognised as the next generation and handled much more easily. For the first few minutes I kept the Moth straight and level. Then I was told to go up to 2,000 feet, watching the altimeter all the time, and circle the airstrip to get the hang of the aileron and rudder controls. My first attempt made me stray off course a little, but I gradually began to feel a part of the plane, and she responded true to my touch. The next move was to start banking the Moth, first to the left, then to the right. Because this was my first flight in a Tiger Moth, the instructor barked out over the radio "Right, bring her in to land. Keep her level, nose up, flaps down, and watch your airspeed!" A few moments later I did a good three-point landing back on the airstrip. My instructor was quite impressed at my overall flying ability, and promised to take me up another day.

The week before Christmas the Pastor had another surprise for me, and asked if I would like to take the Christmas Day Service. It was one that I had seen him conduct for a number of years, so I had a good idea what he would look for. Over the next few days I therefore spent time preparing my address and choosing suitable Christmas hymns. After all that the Pastor had shown me, together with all the theoretical and practical aspects of the course itself, I felt confident enough to do a good job. As the congregation gathered in the church for this special service, I was sure that I saw a few smiles. Perhaps they were still wondering if, after all this time, this big step would be too much for me. This was not the case, though the organist did have a few problems keeping the organ going because of a lack of air pressure. He apologised for this and, like many of the congregation on their way out of the church after the service, congratulated me for the way in which I had conducted it.

CHAPTER 6

As we entered 1935, many people remarked upon the changes in the lives of many around the world. All through the year the newspapers told of the political turmoil in countries like Germany, Italy, and Spain, and Russia, as well as in certain less well-known African countries like Ethiopia, which was attacked by Mussolini's Italian army. It seemed as if the world was turning itself into one large bubble, and it had to burst at some time or other. Even in this country there was unrest. For several years there had been a real depression, and through 1935 unemployment was still running at a staggering twenty per cent. Many families, especially those living in the more heavily-populated areas, were finding it harder and harder to make ends meet. In the United States measures were taken to try and reduce the level of unemployment by creating the 'Emergency Relief Appropriation Act', which was designed as a work-relief program that employed people to build roads, bridges, airports, public buildings and public parks. The President, Franklin D. Roosevelt, also signed the US Social Security Act, which provided unemployment compensation and pensions for the elderly.

Of course, there had to be some good things about 1935 as well. The Penguin publishing company was established in England, producing paperback books that were available at an economical price, and in so doing opening the avenues of reading to many more. Also, the wonderful little cartoon character Mickey Mouse, created by Walt Disney, made his first film in Technicolor, entitled "The Band Concert", in that year. We all enjoyed watching it, and were all laughing at Mickey's efforts to conduct the band whilst being constantly interrupted by his stubborn friend Donald Duck.

At home the Pastor and I had been sharing duties at the church. He had so enjoyed the atmosphere during the services for so long that he found it difficult to stand down at times, and I knew it. There were weeks when his absence caused me to take the services in his stead, but I would not have wished to deny him any less of the life that he described as "in the service of God, yet a servant to the people". Meanwhile Ruth and I had continued to plan a date for our wedding. Eventually it was set for 25th May, and we wanted this to be a real day to remember.

At the beginning of the year Edward had asked us where

we would like to live once we were married, and we replied that we would soon be looking for a house in the village where we had both grown up. At the end of April he called us together with him again, and suddenly presented us with a set of keys. With a tear in his eye, he told us that he had bought us a small two-bedroomed cottage in the village. It had been empty for the last year, and it would be his special wedding present for us. Unknown to me, and because the cottage had needed some modernisation, he had also called upon my father's DIY skills in decorating, carpentry and plumbing. It now looked quite pristine. It was partially furnished, and ready for us, as its new proprietors, to move in. There was a row of tall pine trees on the ridge that we could see not far from the end of the garden. For this reason we named the house 'The Fir Croft', which seemed quite an apt name.

I remembered what my friend Cecil had said to me at the college, and how he had helped give me the confidence to propose to Ruth. For this reason I asked him to come down to the village to be my Best Man. He lived in the city of Birmingham, so it was the first time he had been in this area. He had his own car by this time, and had passed one of the new tests for a driving licence, but he did need a few directions from the locals to get there. It was good to see him again after all this time, and when he arrived during the third week in May my parents offered to let him stay in our spare room, which was a nice thought. Then, as the day drew gradually closer, we checked our preparations over and over again. The great day just wouldn't come fast enough.

On 25th May Cecil drove me to the church for the wedding service, which was timed for 11 am. We both wore our best suits, and I made sure my Best Man had the wedding rings in his pocket. The Marriage Banns had been read over the last few weeks, and news of the wedding had obviously circulated right round the village. Together with my parents, there were many of the church members waiting there to take part in the celebrations. Even my former Principal, Harry Greenaway, turned up at about 10.30 am. As the hour drew closer, the Pastor called me and Cecil to the front, in order to await the coming of the bride. On the hour the organ suddenly went quiet, then started playing the Wedding March. A few moments later, as the church door opened, Ruth entered in her white bridal costume and veil, which had been made specially for the occasion by her mother Alice, carrying a posy of white flowers. Behind her came two bridesmaids, who had been chosen from the village school by the headmistress there. They too wore white dresses. Even though Edward was now confined to a wheelchair, he was pushed up and painfully held his daughter's hand as she walked up the aisle to the front to stand at my side. I don't think anything would have stopped him coming to such a special event!

Edward slowly released Ruth's hand and took his place

in the front row, the joy revealed on his face overcoming all the pain he felt. There are times when events so overcome you that you are hardly aware of what is taking place. That's partly what happened to me. Ruth lifted her veil, and as the Pastor asked both Ruth and me the question regarding our acceptance of our promises and responsibilities to each other in marriage, those short words "I do" meant everything. Our wedding rings were exchanged, and I was in such a dream that I only heard the Pastor announce "…that you be man and wife. You may now kiss the bride." It was a moment that we had waited for a long time to happen, and now it was true.

A few moments later we filed through to the church office in order to sign the Marriage Certificate. Outside the church we then stood for the photographer who had been hired, and Ruth threw her posy to the girls nearby, following the old tradition that whoever catches it would be married next. Once this was done, Cecil acted as our chauffeur and drove us to the reception at the local village hall, which had been brightly decorated for our special day. It was here that congratulations were said and gifts offered, but for those who hadn't been at the church service, there was one thing they were waiting for, which was to see Ruth and me kiss each other as husband and wife. We didn't disappoint them, and great cheers broke out.

Later that afternoon we were driven to the station, having packed a couple of small suitcases, to take the train to the Welsh town of New Quay, where we would spend a few days on our honeymoon. New Quay was a town that went back many years and still had a small fishing fleet of its own. As we stood on the jetty near our hotel we saw an old iron anchor on the quayside, probably a relic from the time when numerous large sailing ships graced the seas. The harbour mouth stood before us with the sun breaking through, just like a doorway into a new life. Ruth laughed and said that it might have opened specially for us, because we were starting our new life together. From the harbour wall we could see small shoals of fish, whilst dolphins and porpoises quickly rose to the surface and dived once again as they swam swiftly along in the seawater, and we spent a short time in a contest trying to predict where the dolphins might appear next. We enjoyed our time together in New Quay, and one kindly old fisherman even offered to take us for a trip on his boat, though this was one thing we had to refuse.

When we returned to our new home in the village we had to organise things a little. Everything seemed to be in a different place from where we wanted it. Over the next few days we also spent time purchasing some of the furniture we still needed. Even though we had some basic items, like beds and cabinets, there were other things like a chest of drawers, bookcase, and a wardrobe that we certainly needed. We also had to stock up on a few utensils and food items for the kitchen. For larger items we had to look a little further afield, in the town of Withenbury, about 10 miles from us. Fortunately there was a large store that dealt in used goods, which saved us a lot of money. Because of the large items we had bought, such as a wardrobe, they offered to deliver our purchases within a few days.

As we settled into The Fir Croft, time seemed to move quickly once again, but we also had to earn our living. Whilst my father and I shared the profits from our air ferry service and I gained a small income from the Pastorate, Ruth took on the job of assistant at the nearby general store. She was a good cook, so she was very familiar with food. Customers sometimes asked her if she had any new recipes. As the autumn drew on, and winter steadily approached, the manager offered us a bag of coal as a special Christmas bonus, telling us that Ruth had given a great impression, and that many of his regular customers had not only befriended her, but recommended her. Since he employed Ruth he told us that his sales had noticeably increased.

That Christmas I once again took the Christmas Day service at the church, and spoke of the gifts that were brought to Jesus by the shepherds and the wise men, and what they represented. The wise men who made their long pilgrimage from the east were astrologers who had seen a new and exceptionally bright star in the sky. They were in no doubt that this represented the birth of a new king, possibly even a Messiah, and they followed the guiding star all the way to the stable where Jesus lay. The shepherds in the fields had heard the angel's message and were overcome with fear when they saw many other angels glorifying God, but were comforted by the angel. Both the wise men and the shepherds had left everything because they believed in the heavenly messages that they had been given, which demonstrated their faith. We too can demonstrate our faith by coming to the Lord Jesus Christ and accepting Him for what He is, our Lord and Saviour, the one who died upon the cross bearing our sin.

As the New Year dawned, we looked at the memories of 1935 that we all held, but we also looked ahead to what might happen. Later in January this country was in mourning for King George V. A medical bulletin was issued on 20th January declaring "The King's life is moving peacefully toward its close." News reports say that the King died soon afterwards, and his eldest son, the Duke of Windsor, became King Edward VIII. Ruth's father soon declared his disgust at the monarch, particularly since he felt it brought dishonour to the name with which he had been christened. Problems loomed almost immediately for the new Sovereign. His proposed marriage to Wallis Simpson, from the United States, aroused much controversy because she had become a divorcee of some reputation. Even those with some authority, including other members of the British Royal Family, described Edward as "nothing but a flirt", and that this country would never accept an American divorcee as a Queen. Also, it was said that the Coronation

Oath was meant to be taken by one who would be seen as the head of the Church of England, yet Edward never went to church. How could he possibly take the Coronation Oath if this were true?

Yet Edward's determination to marry Wallis Simpson seemed unbreakable, and it turned into a struggle between crown and family. In the end, in December 1936, Edward broadcast a radio message to the people that proclaimed "I have found it impossible to carry the heavy burden of responsibility and to discharge my duties as king as I would wish to do without the help and support of the woman I love." On Edward's abdication from the throne his younger brother Albert, Duke of York, took the throne as George VI, probably in honour of his late father, George V. This was the first time since 1066 that Britain had had three different sovereigns in a single year.

Meanwhile, in Germany, Hitler's popularity showed last August at the beginning of the Olympic Games in Berlin, when over 91,000 spectators and competitors were crowded into the new stadium to watch him conduct the opening ceremony. There is an old saying that one cannot judge a book by its cover, and in some ways Hitler's true character still remained a mystery. His supporters idolised him, but others saw him as a threat to peace. Unfortunately the fear that he and his followers in the Nazi party had instilled into the minds of doubters seemed to diminish any active response or opposition to his leadership. One could see this from the military measures that he had already taken. He had sent German troops into the highly industrialised, yet still officially demilitarised, area of the Rhineland. There were also rumours that he had offered the services of the German armed forces to General Franco in Spain, where civil war broke out in July. Unfortunately it was rather like good food - some people, once they get their teeth into it, just don't know where to stop. However, even at this time, it was not for me to start worrying about the future. I knew which way my path was going, and I had no intention of leaving it to pursue what might be thoughts of mere fantasy.

At a church meeting in the autumn I spoke of the political tensions in Germany, and how they resembled those in Palestine at the time of Jesus. Before the Romans first occupied the country, the High Priests and Jewish rulers collaborated to gain favour. Even though the Nationalist Zealots tried to bring about a revolution, and created a thorn in the side of the Roman authorities by doing so, many of their leaders were brought to justice and punished. The Romans saw Jesus as a troublemaker, one who had gained much support through the miracles that he performed, and for this they insisted upon the harshest punishment – crucifixion. Anyone showing dissent in Germany was also likely to be punished.

CHAPTER 7

At the beginning of 1937, everything was going well. Having the responsibilities of the church meant that I had to make visits to families in the area. By that time the winter had eased a little, but it was still very cold, so I suggested to Ruth that we should have our own car. If I learned to drive it would solve the problems of visiting, whilst it would also help to get her to work whenever necessary. One day I wandered along to the new petrol station that had opened in the village, and was greeted by the mechanic Arnold, whom I knew as a loyal church member. I explained my problem to him, and he suddenly declared that he had got just what I needed. He then took me to the back of the garage and showed me a small black car, an Austin Seven from about 1933. He said it had had its rear bumper damaged about six months previously, but added that such parts were relatively easy to obtain, so he could repair it for me and have it on the road within a short time. It seemed a good buy, because the car itself had a low mileage and the engine didn't sound too bad. After such a long time sitting in the shed doing nothing it took a while to crank it up to start, but Arnold said that the engine just needed tuning and then it would be good as new. He also gave me the name of a local driving instructor who would teach me all the aspects of driving a car, together with any other road safety measures I should know.

I soon contacted the instructor and made an appointment for my first driving lesson the following week. During the lesson he explained the basic controls in the car, and I was soon out on the road with him. After a short time he took the passenger seat, explaining road sense, signals and everything else I needed to know. Flying an aircraft was certainly different from this, but with every little practice I became more competent. It wasn't long before my instructor said I would soon be capable enough to take the driving test, and thus qualify for a driving licence. This I did in early March.

In some respects I didn't gain my driving licence a moment too soon. About the third week in March Ruth and I were sharing an evening at home when she suddenly announced that she was pregnant. She had been to see the local doctor, who had confirmed this. Our parents were overjoyed to hear that they would soon have their first grandchild.

There was now a discussion about whether they would prefer a boy or a girl. Our mothers quite definitely wanted a girl, whilst our fathers had other thoughts, declaring that they would be proud to have a boy. We would have to wait and see! Over the following weeks, as the bulge slowly appeared, we all advised Ruth to take things easy, and possibly reduce her hours at the general store. This she did at the end of May, soon after we had celebrated our second wedding anniversary.

I have always been interested in news from around the world, and there are times when my ethical background, as well as the realism that I have to face in my position at the church, simply arouses my curiosity to look deeper into the news. On 20th January 1937 the President of the United States, Franklin D. Roosevelt, was inaugurated for the second time. He had first been inaugurated in 1933 when the signs of the Great Depression could still be seen in the unemployment and poverty throughout the country and, whilst tending to blame banks and other financial institutions for the problem, he also offered suggestions that might help stabilise the country once again. These had some success, and Roosevelt was re-elected with an increased majority in 1936.

As a pilot I was interested to hear about Amelia Earhart's attempt to fly around the world. On 17th March she left Oakland, California on the first leg of her trip to Honolulu, Hawaii with a crew of three on board the large twin-engined Lockheed Electra monoplane. Unfortunately, due to a number of technical problems which included engine lubrication and faults with the propellers, the aircraft was forced to land at the US naval base at Ford Island, Pearl Harbor in Hawaii. The aircraft needed servicing, and the flight resumed three days later. On take-off either a tyre suddenly burst or the undercarriage broke, sending the aircraft into a backward flip, known to pilots as a ground-loop. There was just too much damage for the flight to continue, so the aircraft needed to be shipped by sea to the Lockheed facility in Burbank, California for repairs.

Two months later, on 20th May, Amelia Earhart took off again in the Electra from Oakland, California, for a second effort to fly round the world, this time from West to East. However, during the first leg to Miami, Florida, technical problems once again caused delays. She later took off from Miami with her navigator, Fred Noonan. Her effort to fly around the world failed, but even though the aircraft was plagued with faults, Amelia Earhart and Fred Noonan managed to achieve the longest flight ever, one of 29,000 miles.

Only a few days before Amelia Earhart was due to start her flight another major air disaster took place. The giant German airship 'Hindenburg' had crossed the Atlantic on one of its regular trips. It is understood that the 800-foot-long airship came through some stormy weather over the Atlantic and reached its docking point at the Naval Air Station near Lakehurst, New Jersey on 6th May. As it approached the mooring mast it was still raining but, rather than delay the landing any more, the usual mooring ropes were dropped from the nose. Suddenly the 'Hindenburg' burst into flames and fell from the sky. The drama was recorded on film and the WLS commentator, Herbert Morrison, shouted over the radio "It's burst into flames! It's burst into flames, and it's falling, it's crashing! Watch it! Watch it! Get out of the way! Get out of the way! Get this, Charlie; get this, Charlie! It's fire—and it's crashing! It's crashing terrible! Oh, my! Get out of the way, please! It's burning and bursting into flames; and the—and it's falling on the mooring-mast."

Many of the 97 people on board jumped from the airship gondola, and of these there were 35 fatalities, together with one of the mooring crew who died, with other severe injuries being caused by the terrifying fire and smoke.

As June drew to a close, even my father made history. For the last 20 years he had relied on his old RE8, but even that was beginning to show its age, and Charles spent more and more time on regular repairs and servicing. He had gained a good income from his small air ferry service, and he also had some savings from the farm. For this reason he decided to buy a plane that was a little bigger, yet still needed only a reasonably short area for its take-off. The old biplane aircraft of old were on the way out, and manufacturers were now designing new monoplanes that were said to be faster, more reliable, and even had a pressurized cockpit, which meant that pilots would not have to deal with the very cold air once they were airborne. They would also take bigger loads, which would be ideal.

He made a couple of telephone calls to his friend at the city airfield, who suggested an American-built Curtis Robin. These had first been produced in 1928, when the engine fitted gave little more speed than the Tiger Moth. However, by this time a more powerful engine was being produced, and some American companies were using the Robin for mail and passenger transport. There was room for two passengers in the cockpit with the pilot, so the aircraft provided an extra element of space and comfort. The Robin he bought was a second-hand model from 1933, and certainly wasn't cheap, but he felt it was more of an investment for the future. As well as my Pastoral duties, I looked to increase my flight experience as well.

By August Ruth and I had started making serious preparations for the arrival of our new baby. Even though it wasn't due until December we were already getting a list ready of what we might need. This almost became two lists, one for a girl, one for a boy, because we just didn't know, and even the doctor couldn't tell us. Ruth had already cut her hours at the grocers and in some ways, she was beginning to feel the strain of pregnancy. Fortunately for us there was a former nurse in the village who had worked for a time at a nearby cottage hospital who was able to give us some good advice, for which we were very grateful.

As December approached it seemed as if everyone was eagerly waiting for the baby. Suddenly, on the evening of 7th December, when I was in the armchair reading through the discussion topics for the next church home group, Ruth entered the room with a look of real pain on her face and frantically choked out that the baby was coming. We immediately called Jane, the nurse, who mounted her bicycle without delay, having agreed to act as a midwife. By the time she arrived Ruth was already lying on the bed, but Jane knew exactly what to do. I waited for what seemed like an endless, almost agonizing, period of time, but in the early hours of 8th December Jane opened the door to the bedroom. She smiled, looked at the little bundle of flesh in her arms, and declared "You have a beautiful little daughter!"

As we went back to join Ruth, she handed our new child to me. Since then I have always said that God blessed us, because my daughter just opened her eyes for a moment, gave me a little smile, then went back to sleep in my arms.

That Christmas I almost considered giving a message about Mary and Elizabeth, two mothers of note who were great friends with each other. Mary was the wife of Joseph and the mother of Jesus himself, whilst Elizabeth was the wife of Zechariah and the mother of John the Baptist. It was these two mothers after whom we were going to name our baby daughter. She was now our pride and joy. Ruth had to take life easy for a few days after Mary was born, but Edward and Alice, then Charles and Maria, had the joy of seeing their new granddaughter for the first time. As a special Christmas present, Alice had knitted a little cuddly toy that looked like a small teddy bear. For a girl she had knitted it specially in pink, and little Mary loved it from the moment she set eyes upon it. She took it and grasped it close to herself, just as if it were her own baby. We also set up a small decorated Christmas tree at home. Being only three weeks old, Mary might not have understood the meaning of Christmas just yet, but we could see her small blue eyes looking carefully at the tree, taking in all the little decorations on it and the presents around it. We certainly expected her to know what would happen when next year came around.

As the New Year approached we had our traditional family party, when Alice cooked a special turkey. It had to be held at Ruth's parents' home because Edward's condition had deteriorated so much with the cold weather that he was now virtually housebound, and we were quite concerned, not only for him, but also for Alice, who had become his full-time carer. However, Ruth and I did have our own little memories as we kissed under the mistletoe once again.

CHAPTER 8

As 1938 began there was already disquiet rumbling through the world. The Japanese government had claimed that areas of China, particularly Manchuria, were in fact Japanese territory, which the Chinese Nationalists totally rejected. Japan, being an island nation, had always relied on raw materials from outside, and since much of the territory in Asia was a part of the great world empires they probably decided to take matters into their own hands. Chinese cities were bombed, whilst Japanese land forces invaded eastern parts of China. The Japanese claimed that it was the Chinese who fired the first shots, but no one is sure about that.

In March, Hitler's troops marched into Austria and declared an 'Anschluss' or union, which meant that Austria was no longer an independent country but merely a state of the new Germanic Empire. Hitler himself was of Austrian birth, and many of the population had German relatives, so they too decided to support the Nazi cause. This was a country that had been a part of the Austro-Hungarian Empire which had been dismembered at the end of the Great War, and it had fought with Germany, so overall there was little resistance to the occupation of the country. The newsreel films showed Hitler in an open top car parading through the streets of Vienna before a madly waving, cheering crowd.

Even Benito Mussolini, the plump dictator of fascist Italy, made a name for himself. There had been objections to Italy's occupation of Abyssinia, but soon political sources were making efforts to have the new fascist government in Abyssinia recognized.

These were only a few of the areas of conflict or disquiet throughout the world. I certainly didn't remember it having created so much anxiety, even in our area. There were those who believed that there could be another, even more disastrous conflict than the Great War not far ahead. Some preparatory measures were already being taken around our country. The previous year a national group called Air Raid Precautions (ARP) had been started. After the city of Guernica was bombed during the Spanish Civil War there was a feeling that if any conflict came to this country then we should have trained volunteers there as Air Raid

Wardens to take charge, their job being to warn of any approaching air raids and organize the movement of other civilians to the nearest air raid shelters. The group was made up of a growing number of civilians who might not be eligible to serve as regular troops in any conflict, but still wanted to play an active part.

At first the Pastor was a little wary of allowing me too much responsibility in the church. He still had a premonition that war was coming, and he also felt that I still had an urge to fly, but how this would affect me I did not yet know. Although I took a number of the regular Sunday services, there were times when he preferred to use me simply as a Reader. I read the scriptural text whilst he gave the sermon. I must admit, to be put on the shelf like that did make me feel a little uncomfortable at times. Perhaps it was my youth, and the Pastor wanted to give me more time either to settle in or make a decision as to what I needed to do.

Once the weather had cleared after the cold winter, my father resumed his air transport service. He realised that the distributors of various goods were anxious to get their products on sale as quickly as possible. They found that by using Charles' air transport service rather than the long, monotonous road trips, they could extend the range of their business. Items such as fresh food needed to be delivered promptly, and Charles could do this by using the growing number of flying clubs around the country. There were also occasions when he could arrange a second delivery, or collect passengers, from his first point of call. This meant that much of his day was taken up with flying, but he gained a good reputation with a profitable business. I think my father appreciated the fact that I no longer had just my duties at the church but extra duties at home to carry out whilst Ruth was getting back to normal, and whilst little Mary was still in infancy. For this reason he employed on part-time work a young trainee pilot named Jacob. Even though there were days when I still managed to carry out some of the shorter deliveries, there were occasions when Charles took Jacob along as his co-pilot. If the delivery meant long flying hours, then one could take a short break in the cockpit whilst the other took control of the Curtis. Doing it this way meant that neither got over-tired. It also enabled Jacob to gain plenty of experience before he took his final pilot's test.

Meanwhile, we did have a tragedy at home. We had known for a long time that Edward's arthritis was crippling him, and there were signs that it was becoming too much for him. Eventually, in September, he passed away at home with his family beside him. Edward had been a true father figure, one who gave his all so that we might reap the benefits, and that reminded me of Jesus, who had died on the cross at Calvary to set us free from the burden of sin. He was one who had served his King and Country with honour, and had often faced death in the battlefield trenches of the Great War, where many had said that if there was a bullet with your name on it, then that would be that. Edward had learned not to fear death but to do his duty as a soldier through it. It was different with the arthritis, where it was more of a long, slow ending, but he faced it with courage, even though he knew there could only be one outcome. We only wished that he had known his granddaughter for a little longer. Had he had the chance to see her grow up, then we believe that would have made his joy complete.

The funeral service took place at the end of the month, and the Pastor allowed me to conduct it. Edward himself had said that if or when anything happened to him he didn't want a church full of miserable people grieving for him, and this was one of the reasons why we chose the hymn "Fight the good fight". We felt that this matched his character both as a soldier and a Christian. Ruth gave her own tribute during the service, and once we left the church his body was interred in the churchyard.

At the end of the month, when Edward's will was read, we found that he had given a large share to us, but he had also left a share for Alice, probably because he knew she would find it difficult to gain any income. The family house was left in trust so that Alice might live there for the rest of her life. However, Alice herself suggested that because the house had several bedrooms, the three of us might consider moving in. We could then rent out our own cottage and earn an income from that. We found that the gardener and his wife who were working at the large country house a few miles away desperately needed accommodation and, having no children of their own, the cottage would be ideal for them.

That month news also went around of the Munich Conference. At the beginning of October we heard news reports about the unrest in Czechoslovakia. A number of German-speaking families in the area known as the Sudetenland had shown support for Hitler. Last April the leader of the Sudeten Germans demanded self-government. This so alarmed the official Czech Government under Eduard Benes that he called up reservists and positioned troops to guard the German border. Having condemned this provocative action, Hitler himself was now echoing the demands of the Sudeten Germans. The British Prime Minister, Neville Chamberlain, was one of those trying to persuade Eduard Benes to make concessions. Hitler, to make matters worse, declared that a large number of German troops had been massed along the border. All it needed was a little spark and everything would go up in smoke. At the Munich Conference the leaders of Germany, Italy, France and Britain essentially decided the fate of Czechoslovakia and its new borders, though it was strange that none of the Czech leaders were present at the conference. The newsreels were showing footage of the Czech evacuation and the entry of the Germans to the sound of triumphant music. Chamberlain may have considered that we needed more time to rearm in the event of war, so his policy of appeasement may not have been popular, but it certainly gave us extra time. How long did we have? He flew back from Munich with a non-aggression treaty signed by Adolf Hitler and displayed it to everyone, declaring "Peace in our time."

In December we celebrated little Mary's first birthday. We made up a few decorations for the house, and the baker supplied us with an iced cake with the number 1 written on it in a different coloured icing. Because she was still so young we didn't really miss a lighted candle, and it would be safer in the end. Even though she was only a child, I think she recognized that this was a special day for her. It was also difficult in the sense that her birthday and Christmas were so close together, so we decided to watch her birthday presents. If there were too many then we could put a couple by for Christmas under the usual Christmas tree. We knew it would probably be our last Christmas in The Fir Croft, because early the following year we would be moving in with Alice. Mary would certainly be able to see her grandmother a lot more.

Mary joined us at the Christmas Day Service for the first time. I was now always speaking at these services, but that year I tried something different. I spread word around the village that any children who came should bring one of their Christmas presents. By doing this it would enable the younger generation of churchgoers to take part and to feel a bigger part of the church. A number of parents brought their children to church, and we set them carefully in a line at the front. I then went down the line, asking the children what their presents were, and added at the end that all the children had been good enough to receive gifts, but that there was one gift that only our faith in the Lord Jesus could bring about. Several of the congregation remarked that they considered the involvement of the children to be a good idea, and perhaps one that could be repeated next year.

Later that day Ruth and I put some flowers on Edward's grave in the churchyard, which was covered in snow from the recent winter weather. It was a simple wreath, but it was in memory of one whom we would never forget.

CHAPTER 9

At the end of January 1939, once the Christmas rush was over, we started to make preparations to move in with Alice. She had kept some of Edward's treasures as a memento. There was his collection of wartime medals, many of his favourite books, and also a small stamp collection. As mail services had flourished across the world, many more countries were producing their own stamps and, before the arthritis had crippled him, one of Edward's hobbies had been to contact many of his old friends, some of whom now lived in other areas of the British Empire, and request a set of stamps from the countries where they lived. It was a hobby that not only helped his stamp collection to grow but enabled him to renew and maintain contact with old friends and veterans of the Great War, some of whom he had not seen for a long time. Alice also had a large photo album in which she kept all the photos that she and Edward had taken together during their long years of marriage.

We needed a means of transporting all our goods from The Fir Croft, though we left much of our furniture there so it could be used by our new tenants, the gardener and his wife. Some of the smaller items, like our own photos, Mary's clothes, and all the goods for our personal needs we crammed into the back of my Austin Seven car, but because of its small size we also had to hire a van. Arnold, who was still running the garage, helped us out once again by supplying one of his own vehicles.

Eventually our move was complete, and we settled into what was to be our new home. It wasn't really new, because Ruth had grown up in it, and we had spent much time together there. Our only problem was one of our bathroom mirrors, which had unexpectedly moved in the van and then had something fall on it. We had to visit the general store to buy another one, together with something to hang it on the wall, a job which I later completed without too much difficulty.

Meanwhile I still had other duties to perform at the church. Because of the cold weather the Pastor had caught a severe chill and was resting at the rectory. We all offered to help in whatever way possible. He couldn't eat much at first, so we had to treat him carefully using the old method of lemon juice and boiling water in a mixing bowl. He covered his head with a towel and leaned over the bowl to inhale the warm, refreshing lemon-scented air. It was several days before he started getting over the chill, and about two weeks before he took part in limited duties at the church. This meant that I had to prepare the Sunday services several weeks running, as well as running our home group. It almost gave me a taste of what full-time Pastoral work could be like, but I think I managed quite capably.

One thing I learned was how to deal with children, because there was one mischievous child who was always interrupting the service. She was only five years old, so she may have done it quite unknowingly, but I still had to ask her mother to keep a close eye on her. There were times when visits were necessary to see families or individuals with needs or problems. Having someone understanding to talk to often eased their minds and helped them take a more positive stance.

We had to take a positive attitude with all the threats coming from abroad. General Franco, the leader of the revolutionary group in Spain, had taken full control of the government, and the United States had decided to recognize this government. There was also news that Italy had invaded Albania and that Hitler had occupied the remaining area of Czechoslovakia without warning. There was still war in the Far East as well. The League of Nations, founded by the American President Woodrow Wilson in 1918 to try and unite more nations to help prevent war, seemed to have failed miserably. Several countries, including Italy and Germany, had already left to form their own alliance, initially known as the Rome-Berlin Axis alliance, later the Pact of Steel. Soon after this Hitler made dramatic claims that he wanted to move into Poland. No wonder Poland was mobilizing its army. There were also rumours that Hitler had approached the government of Japan and invited them to become members of the Axis. Others were also considering leaving the League of Nations. Many were concerned that the threat of war in this country was growing.

We were lucky to have politicians from other countries who had the same ideas as us. In April we signed a military pact with Poland, and even the leader of communist Russia, Josef Stalin, requested that Great Britain, France and Russia should sign an anti-Nazi pact.

It may sound as if I had nothing better to dwell on than world politics, but that was certainly not the case. I wasn't much of a sportsman myself, but there were some exceptional sporting champions around. Look at Joe Louis, the black heavyweight boxer who successfully defended his world title several times. Being a man of speed in the air, I also thought of John Cobb, who set a new land speed record of 365.85 mph over the measured mile at Bonneville Flats in America. I wonder what it feels like to be travelling at that speed.

Almost exactly three weeks after we celebrated Ruth's

birthday on 10th August, the bubble suddenly burst. For some reason Stalin seemed to go back on his word by signing a non-aggression pact with Hitler, who at last decided to carry out his threats against the Poles. The newsreels showed joyful German soldiers breaking down the barriers at the Polish border.

Our Sunday service on 3rd September was supposed to start at 11 am, but the Pastor had to delay it because of an important announcement that was being broadcast by the Prime Minister at that time. He also arranged for a radio in the church so that the congregation could hear the message without having to return home. The radio was switched on just before 11 am, but nothing new was announced at first. Then, at about 11.15, everyone stopped to listen to Neville Chamberlain's announcement that Hitler had openly defied any request to withdraw his troops from Poland. He added in a sombre voice "Consequently this country is at war with Germany." The person next to me remarked "So, it's happened at last!"

For some time war had seemed inevitable, and a few preparations were being made. At the beginning of the war, all civilians were issued with gas masks. The government remembered the use of poison gas by the Germans during the Great War, and feared that this might happen again, possibly even on a larger scale, with poison gas being dropped during aerial attacks. Even though they had begun the issue of gas masks last July, together with a manual on their fitting and use, many civilians had still not received them by September. The gas mask that had been issued for little Mary was a cumbersome old thing that was almost big enough for her to fit inside. In the cities bomb shelters were being built, whilst smaller Anderson shelters were being provided for individual families. Black-out times were also introduced, and curtains or blinds had to be kept drawn. Any sign of light from a house would immediately get a shout of "Put that light out!" from the patrolling warden.

One of the first things to be rationed was petrol, or motor spirit as the government called it. It was felt that the armed forces needed as much fuel as they could get, and rationing was introduced because all our petrol supplies came from overseas. Unless it was used for what the government called 'special purposes', we were only allowed from 4-10 gallons per month. We all guessed that this was likely to decrease as the war went on. Though it didn't affect me too much, because I still only had my Austin Seven, it was quite a blow to my father, because after a short while all his supplies dried up, and his air transport service was forced to close. He had built his own hangar for the old RE8, which he still treasured, but the Curtis Robin was another matter. He turned to the flying club where he had originally bought the Robin, and they agreed to temporarily store the aircraft in one of their own hangars. It wasn't exactly big, but the club had a number of other small planes, one of which would fill up the space in the same hangar.

However, the problem did not only concern the aircraft. Closing the service meant that Jacob would need to find other employment, and Charles himself had to look elsewhere to gain some sort of income for his own and Maria's everyday needs. Other resources needed to be found promptly. He was fortunate enough to have his farm with the beef cattle, some of which he could sell on to make a profit, but he knew they would not last forever. One suggestion was that he might breed rabbits in one corner of the field. Poachers had always found them easy to catch and worth selling on to those who wanted a decent Sunday meal. There was even a recipe for a Christmas meal described as 'Mock Turkey', but actually made from rabbit. I felt sure Charles would see the demand for rabbits caused by Bud Flanagan's song 'Run, Rabbit, Run!' increase, and construct some sort of pen where he could keep and breed his rabbits.

Once food rationing started for real, he had to consider other tactics as well. Posters all around the nearby towns encouraged people to "Dig for Victory", and those with no garden even grew vegetables in window boxes, so my father decided that once the spring came he would borrow his neighbour's plough for a few days. With luck he would be able to plant some seed potatoes and with the area of land he had available, he believed this could be beneficial in every way. Not only would he be providing food for himself and my mother, he could once again sell it on at a profit.

He also had second thoughts about Jacob, and asked if

he would be willing to stay on and help him with the farm. Jacob agreed, on condition that he could be released if he was called up for National Service. He was still only 17 years old, so it would be no more than 18 months or so before he was called up.

The plough itself was only a single-furrow affair that needed a horse to draw it, so it took rather longer than expected. The old shire horse tended to drift from the line we wanted, but if we tried to bring it back on the right line, the horse just relieved itself, adding a touch of good fertiliser to the soil! I pitched in with them to help out and at the end of the day I didn't know how the horse felt, but my muscles were quite stiff from all the work we had done.

We still heard of various criminal activities that were going on. A worker from the Cadbury factory near Birmingham was calling on householders with a squeaky old trolley that contained a full sack of sugar. He said the company had been trying to reduce the sugar content of some of their products, so he didn't consider that they needed it any more!

Because of the threat of bombing raids, there was an influx of evacuees from the city, most of whom were children. Families who had any spare rooms were invited to have a child to live with them. Some families welcomed another child, while others accepted them a little more cautiously. We were allowed to have a little girl called Ruby, who is seven years old, and whose parents live in Bristol.

Having met little Mary, now nearly two, Ruby said she would love to be her big sister.

A local builder added that he had a number of large wooden panels which had been used in the construction of barns, declaring that he could construct a large frame set a few inches above the ground, and covered by panels that had been lined to keep in the heat. A floor would be made of standard size planks, a slate roof could be fitted over a suitably constructed frame, and temporary water and power services could be installed. He called it a pre-fabricated building or 'prefab' for short, and said it could be constructed and completed in a few days. It might act as a temporary home, but I didn't think the idea would catch on. With all the new children in the village Alice started helping out in the school once again.

In some respects the atmosphere was strange and a little hard to understand. This was our first wartime Christmas, but in many of the less-affected rural areas of the country it was spent as if there had been no problems or changes at all. I suppose it was considered morale-boosting. Probably the urban areas felt the restrictions more, because we had large areas of land where we could always grow or produce our own food.

The King gave out his Christmas Broadcast over the radio. He had a stammer, which he tried to overcome by hesitating a little in between phrases. This too acted as a good morale-booster. We believe he was dressed as an

Admiral of the Fleet to broadcast the message from his desk at Sandringham, which began: "A new year is at hand. We cannot tell what it will bring. If it brings peace, how thankful we shall all be. If it brings us continued struggle, we shall remain undaunted." Overall the message was one of encouragement for all, yet there was a need for caution under the circumstances.

CHAPTER 10

At the beginning of February 1940 I was told by an RAF serviceman that there was not only a shortage of aircraft, particularly the new monoplane fighters which had been developed to match the enemy Messerschmitt Bf109, but a shortage of skilled pilots as well. We had sent troops across the Channel in 1939 to make up what was called the BEF, or British Expeditionary Force. They could not have been very comfortable dug in on the French border, and up to then the weather had been so cold that neither we nor the Nazi forces had taken any offensive action, hence the reason why we had nicknamed this period the Phoney War. Yet there was almost a sense of foreboding in the air. Something was bound to happen once the weather improved, but we had no idea what, where or when.

I wondered what Ruth would think if I joined the RAF, especially now that we had Mary, Elizabeth and Ruby to look after. The Bible says: "When a man hath taken a new wife, he shall not go out to war, neither shall he be charged with any business; but he shall be free at home one year, and shall cheer up his wife which he hath taken." (Deuteronomy 24:5). However, we had seen that year through and were happy with each other, so I wanted it to be a joint decision rather than just mine.

Even though it was a hard decision, both we and our parents felt that unless we did something to uphold the Christian freedom and beliefs that this country had always stood for, we might succumb to the terror and fear that the Nazis had already imposed upon the population of Germany and other countries they had occupied. Even the old Pastor appreciated my position, so he agreed for me to be temporarily reassigned to war duties. He promised to cope until my return once the hostilities had ended. However, before I left to join up, a special time of prayer was held during the church service on the following Sunday. I told the congregation that this was a war where everyone had to do their bit. I would not be leaving them permanently, because this church was an important part of my life. However, I had skills that could be used to do my duty to King and Country.

That Tuesday I walked in to the local RAF Enlistment Bureau. I couldn't be a part of the regular RAF, and the

Auxiliary Air Force didn't seem right, but there were still a few places available in the RAF Volunteer Reserve, which I had been told would be the source of many replacement fighter pilots. The first question was easy enough -
"Why do you want to join the RAF?" I replied that I could fly and wanted to join as a pilot. Then I was asked, "What sort of pilot do you want to be, fighter, bomber or reconnaissance?" I responded that I wanted to be a fighter pilot. The officer continued "Why do you want to be a fighter pilot in particular?" and to this I replied that I was already a skilled pilot with experience of both biplanes and monoplanes, and also that my father was an ex-RFC pilot who had taken the time to instruct me on some of the general formation flying and combat tactics from the Great War. I believe the enlistment officer was quite impressed. After going through all the red tape of the enlistment process, such as additional paperwork, medical examination, and issue of uniform, I was posted without delay to one of the Reserve Flight Training Units near the city of Birmingham.

Imagine my surprise when I arrived and reported to the Commanding Officer as a new Cadet, only to find that the CO was my old flying instructor with the Tiger Moth. I imagine he was considered to be too old for combat duties, and the Tiger Moth was still used as one of the RAF's primary training aircraft, and with his experience flight training would be an ideal position for him. He explained to me that because of my flying hours, which were about 140 on biplanes and 28 on the Curtis monoplane, so long as I could demonstrate my ability to a good standard he might consider reducing the total number of weeks that the flight training covered. The course usually took anything up to 17 weeks, but he believed that with my previous experience he could reduce this to about 10 weeks.

During the first week the emphasis was on general flight instructions, formations and a look at aircraft identification, as well as being taught how to salute and march, which seemed an endless process. Even at this stage I could see how much aerial warfare had changed over the years since the Great War. Instead of rickety biplanes we had fast, well-armed monoplane fighters and powerful bombers that could take a heavier bomb load, as well as having a longer range.

During the second week we were taken out to the Tiger Moths parked on the airstrip and given instructions about the controls. The CO then asked me to take the pilot's seat and whispered in my ear "Now, show them what can be done with a Moth". This was just a little more than the usual circuit and bumps that new pilots would do, so I cautiously asked which manoeuvres he expected from me. The simple answer was "Give it the works!" The CO knew how long I had spent with him in a Tiger Moth, and knew I could carry out manoeuvres that might not be in a new pilot's thoughts.

I taxied out onto the airstrip and went through the usual pre-flight checks – power on, check rudder, ailerons working, flaps down, then full throttle -   it was just like being part of a giant bird. A moment later the nose came up and the Moth lifted gracefully into the sky. Once the flaps were up I first did a simple circuit around the airfield to get the feel of the plane again, but as I approached the field next time I put the Moth into a couple of barrel rolls. The plane seemed to be responding perfectly to my touch. Next time around I went into one of the tactics from the Great War my father had shown me, known as the 'Immelmann loop'. This was a combat tactic named after the German ace Max Immelmann, who first used it when an enemy aircraft attacked from behind to gain height and turn to dive in behind his pursuer, thus changing from a defensive to an offensive role.

I felt that was enough for one session, so I brought the Moth in to land - check rudder, flaps down, throttle back to cut the airspeed, nose up   -   a beautiful three-point landing. I taxied back to where the CO and other cadets were standing, and I could see that the CO had a smile on his face. I took my flying helmet off and climbed out onto the ground.

As we looked into some of the more modern combat tactics over the next few days, such as which way to break if one's formation was attacked, some of the cadets were a little envious of me, but I quietly reassured them that I had had two good teachers, including the CO, and that it wouldn't be long before they could do just the same.

Time was also spent getting experience of the radio sets that one now found in modern fighters. We had to imitate making and receiving calls using the Link trainer that was available. One of us would represent the pilot, another would represent Ground Control. The Link was merely a plane simulator, but it gave us all a good chance to get used to the extra controls that we would find in a modern fighter. Later, some of the cadets found that their ability to use the flight controls would be tested on the Link trainer before they were allowed to fly solo.

Because they found the controls more complicated or more difficult to understand than they first imagined, some of the cadets turned to other posts as air or ground crew. Sandy Cook, who had done some hunting on his father's farm, went into air gunnery, whilst Dusty Miller, who before the war was an amateur radio ham, took the radio operator's course. I heard that they found it much more to their liking.

Some six weeks after I joined the RAF, there came the distressing news that enemy forces had now invaded the Scandinavian countries. They seemed to take the offensive and advanced quickly, overcoming any resistance that the Norwegians could throw at them. Even our own troops seemed to be pulling out. Things certainly did not look good there. Since the war had started, much had been said about all the leaflets our bombers had dropped over Germany in a vain effort to try and pacify the situation and warn the enemy what might happen if the conflict were to continue. It appeared they were taking no any notice at all. There were remarks that many were losing faith in Neville Chamberlain, whose errors and pacifist attitude had done nothing for this country.

Meanwhile we tried out the two-seater Miles Magister monoplane trainer, which was seen as a transition between the slower planes we had started off with and the new, faster fighters we expect to fly. It was nearly twice as fast as the Tiger Moth, and still had a fixed undercarriage, but one could certainly tell the difference. The first three hours I spent with my instructor in the back seat, carefully watching all my moves, but I soon did my first solo. I was expected to complete about 175 hours of flying time before I moved up, and I had already completed over 170 hours. Unfortunately one idiot made a foolish bet that he could do a roll in the Tiger Moth at low altitude (and I mean low). Half-way through the manoeuvre he caught his wing on the ground and crashed. He was pretty badly injured, and it was clear the RAF would not want him for any more flying duties. As for the others who made the bet, they were severely reprimanded by the CO.

By May I was in line for my pilot's wings, which had to be stitched onto my uniform. Embroidery wasn't exactly easy for me, so I decided to ask Ruth or Alice to do it when I got my next leave. The CO and main flying instructor took me to see a Hurricane fighter for the first time. It was quite a sleek aircraft, though still made partly of wood and fabric. I was told that many RAF Hurricane squadrons had been upgrading, but for a Training Unit the Hurricane Mark 1 was an ideal plane for new fighter pilots to try. The Merlin engine gave the aircraft a maximum speed of about 318 mph, but the old two-bladed propeller still gave it a touch of age.

The big day came when it was time for my instructor, in another Hurricane, to give me some practice formation flying, and also some practical experience of combat tactics. For the first time I was really going to be a fighter pilot. We went out to the hangar about 11 am, and the ground crew already had the Hurricane ready. My flying suit and helmet seemed light in comparison to what my father used to wear in the Great War. There were pictures of him wrapped thickly with fur-lined jacket, lined boots, thickly-lined leather trousers, helmet and warm gloves. There was no room for a parachute in those days!

As I climbed into the cockpit I was given a few pre-flight instructions, and under my breath I muttered the pre-flight checks that had been drummed into us over the last few weeks. BTFCPPUR - Brakes, Trim, Flaps, Contacts, Pressure (Pneumatic), Undercarriage, Radiator - All clear. It was to be a short flight of about an hour, which would give me time to familiarise myself with the controls and try a few circuits around the airfield. Once that was done the instructor would join me in formation at a given height, and we would try a few combat tactics, though I still wasn't quite sure what his intentions were.

I gave the ground crew the thumbs up sign from the cockpit, pressed the starter button, hand pump working, and suddenly the big Merlin engine roared into life. Chocks away, let's go! Brakes off, increase throttle, not too much... I suddenly felt the Hurricane jerk forward, and I was on my way. I needed to taxi slowly to the end of the airstrip and turn, then check rudder, check flaps, full throttle. The aircraft lifted into the air with the minimum of effort, and I soon levelled out to try the usual circuit. First time round the speed was quite enthralling, but next time I put the flaps down and slowed up to try a landing. Mustn't forget to put the undercarriage down!

Unfortunately my approach was rather fast, and the Hurricane bounced a couple of times, which wasn't good. I opened up the throttle again to gain height, because I had orders over the radio to rejoin formation with my instructor at a given altitude. I was also told to look out for his plane because of the wisps of cloud at that height. At first I was concerned, because I couldn't see his plane anywhere, but then over the radio I suddenly heard a voice imitating a machine-gun as his Hurricane dived past me. I immediately broke left with the rudder hard round, because the Hurricane's turning circle was excellent, but as I came round I saw the second Hurricane gaining height in front of me and the flying instructor barking over the radio "Never fly straight and level for more than 30 seconds. You'll be a sitting duck!" So that was the special combat tactic he had planned for me.

After nearly an hour in the cockpit I was given orders to land, which was a relief, because the cockpit wasn't exactly oversized. This time I got my approach speed just right, and nearly carried out an ideal three-point landing, which I was pleased about. I admitted that my first attempt hadn't been good, but the ground crew were relatively sympathetic, declaring that most new pilots did just the same.

We then received some terrible news from France. The Germans had attacked on 10th May and were driving all before them in an attack through the Low Countries. First of all their dive-bombers came over to silence any tanks, armoured transport or artillery posts, then they sent their own tanks through the gaps in our defences, followed promptly by their infantry forces. This was what they called Blitzkrieg, or lightning war, and the tactics were similar to those used in the invasion of Norway and Denmark. All our boys were struggling to hold them, and it looked as if it would not be long before we would have to retreat and, if necessary, evacuate our troops from France. Some of the coastal ports were already in German hands, and the only one that we seemed to be holding on to was Dunkirk. The squadrons over there were doing what they could to delay the German advance, but planes like the Boulton-Paul Defiant, whose only armament was four machine-guns in a heavy rotating turret at the rear, weren't much good against the fast Me109 fighters armed with both forward-firing cannon and machine-guns.

I needed some more hours in the Hurricane to build up my confidence and evaluate the different controls. I had now done about 15 hours in the Hurricane, with regular flights, so I hoped it wouldn't be long before I got posted to a Combat Squadron so that I could apply all the theory and practical experience I had had. Yet combat is not a situation in which to take things for granted, and those who had already seen combat would be able to give us a few tips.

I was given 48 hours' leave, during which time Ruth and I were able to celebrate our fifth wedding anniversary. Before I left I spoke to the CO, who for once actually showed signs of emotion. He told me to remember all that he and my father had taught me, because it would stand me in good stead. He wished me well, and said to take care, because the Germans really had their tails up. I shook hands with him, saluted smartly, and left his office.

CHAPTER 11

June certainly didn't start off well for us. Our postings were delayed but, most important of all, we saw all the news reports about the evacuation of British and French troops who had been trapped on the beaches at Dunkirk, under constant air attack. We heard of the hundreds of little ships that were used to bring troops back home or, in other cases ferry them to the awaiting destroyers, a number of which were lost. Many more were brought back safely than Churchill, who took over as Prime Minister in mid-May, actually expected. However, the troops could only bring back what they could carry with them, so all our vehicles and artillery had to be abandoned in France. Churchill, who was an old warrior, made a speech declaring, "What General Weygand called the Battle of France is over. The Battle of

Britain is about to begin," and added in his own forceful way "We will never surrender!" We hoped he would be right.

On 10th June I was posted to one of the fighter squadrons in RAF 13 Group, which covered most of the north of England, together with any attacks that might come from the North Sea. The chap who was posted there with me, Jens Fredrikson, was an escaped Norwegian pilot. We met the CO, who asked us both how many hours we'd had in Hurricanes, and our Flight Commander, James 'Jimmy' Whiteside, who was easy to get on with, but stressed that he would personally discipline anyone disobeying or ignoring orders given to them in the air. He told us the story of two replacement pilots who had been with him over France providing some sort of air cover during the Dunkirk evacuation. They saw what looked like a stray Heinkel He111 bomber heading toward Dunkirk and decided to take it on themselves, in spite of being told otherwise. They got a few shots in on the bomber, only to find that it was a trap, and they either ignored or failed to see two formations of Me109 fighters diving on them. One guy ploughed straight into the bomber, and the other's plane was so full of cannon shells that he couldn't even make it back across the Channel. Officially we were 'B' Flight, but unofficially, because our first names all began with the same letter, we were nicknamed 'The Jay Flight'.

For the first few days we rather tuned our skills on the Hurricanes. The two-bladed propeller on the majority of the old Mark 1 planes had been changed to the more efficient three-bladed propeller, which added an extra 10 mph to the plane's maximum speed. The armament had also increased from four to eight Browning .303 calibre machine guns in the wings. These were set to converge at about 250 yards, but there were complaints that half the bullets fired at this distance wouldn't even hit the target. For this reason we reset the range to 200 yards, which meant that if we have a couple of extra seconds to approach the target then we could bring a more concentrated fire upon the enemy. There were also practice scrambles, because we needed to get all our planes airborne in as short a time as possible.

In some respects the atmosphere was very strange. We lived together, ate together, flew together, and at some time we knew we would have to fight together, but to each one the person standing next to him remained a stranger. We anticipated losses, so if anyone got shot down then the rest of the squadron would not get too emotional over the loss. Our emotions had to be re-channelled into our task, to destroy the enemy. It was best like that. The worst part was the waiting, but the Germans had now even occupied the Channel Islands, so we felt something had to happen soon.

France surrendered on 22nd June, but it was a relief to know that some of the Free French forces had escaped to fight with us. A squadron of Free French pilots was posted to a nearby base. Most had been rescued with the troops during the evacuation from Dunkirk, but one had actually been brought back whilst sitting on the lap of a Hurricane pilot when the French airfields were evacuated and all the planes recalled to England. Some of the pilots spoke very good English, which was to work in my favour.

As often occurs, my childhood had not all been rosy. I and my friends from the school run by Alice and Edward were taunted by older children from the classier town school. We were labelled as "incompetent village kids", and one teenager even described us as "incapables who would learn more in a lunatic asylum". I was haunted by the memory of this, and while there were those who did stray from the straight and narrow, I vowed at the age of 12 that I would prove my ability throughout life, so that I could never again be degraded in the same way. In life, everything to me became a can-do. That was one of the reasons why I requested permission to visit the French squadron. One thing I wanted to do was to learn the French language. In the end this decision was to prove more valuable than I had ever guessed.

At the end of June, I had a letter from Ruth. More foods had been rationed, and it could be a little hard with Mary and Ruby to cope with. However, the whole village community seemed to be piling in together to provide help where it was needed, which was good. Some folks were even digging up some of their old country and herbal recipes. The Pastor sent his best wishes, and told me to keep my eyes upon Jesus and pursue my faith in Him every day. He also reminded me of the Old Testament story of King Saul. Saul had been anointed king over Israel, and God charged him with the destruction of the wicked Amalekites, which he duly carried out. Unfortunately, in so doing, Saul started looking at the world and trusting in his own ability, rather than keeping his eyes fixed on God. The prophet Samuel declared that because Saul had rejected God, so God would reject Saul as king. (1 Samuel 15)

A good number of American supplies were now being sent through in convoys, but the Germans were only attacking a few of them, mainly with their Junkers Ju87 Stuka dive bombers. We were told that these had a definite flaw in their design. The only armament at the back was a single machine-gun. Also, as the Stuka pulled out of a dive, its speed would drop tremendously and the gunner's view was limited, making it much easier to pick off.

There were a few heavier raids on coastal towns as well, though the changeable weather hindered them. We thought they wanted to tempt us out on air cover in order to either test our air forces with a view to weakening them gradually, but we were not going to fall for that trick. Following several reports of intruders, we were scrambled, but most of the reports were false alarms. At 13 Group the intruders were more likely to be reconnaissance planes. However, the Germans seemed to be preparing for something big.

I sent Ruth a special card for her birthday on 10th August. Our postal services seemed to be getting worse, so

I hoped she would receive it in time. I also sent a short letter to my parents. The recommendation was that we should just tell people we are fit, eating well, and look forward to seeing them again. It was a load of waffle, really, but there were so many posters around telling us not to give out any information that might be of use to the enemy.

Sometimes it seemed as if the enemy were using Ruth's birthday as a special date themselves. War had been declared three weeks after her birthday in 1939, and on her birthday in 1940 there were reports of swarms of enemy bombers heading for the English coast. There had already been some sporadic raids, most of which 11 Group, the fighter sector covering the south-east, dealt with quite successfully, but now the dive-bombers began attacking one of our main lines of defence, the Radio Direction Finding Stations, which gave us warning against approaching bombers. Some of the main radar stations were damaged or disabled, but at least we still had the Observer Corps to rely on.

On 15th August we were on duty with another squadron. The weather was not too good for summer. As soon as the scramble bell was heard, we ran to our Hurricanes, where members of the ground crew were already waiting. "Where's my parachute? Right, all clear, power on, chocks away, and let's get moving. This is for real!"

Everyone in our flight was ready, so the Flight Commander gave us the signal to take off. Full throttle, and we were airborne, and in good time too. All our practice had paid off. The signal came through from Ground Control - "Phoenix squadron. Enemy aircraft heading south. Angels 10, Vector 085". This gave us the height that we should climb to, together with the compass bearing. Then another message "Phoenix squadron. Enemy aircraft dead ahead, distance five miles, turning west, vector 010 to intercept" Our Flight Commander suddenly declared "Bombers at 10 o'clock. Here we go, boys! Tally ho!"

We all turned in line astern behind the Heinkel He111 bombers on the port side. Blue Section, of which I was a part, attacked the bombers coming in to port, whilst Red Section attacked the centre group and Yellow Section attacked the starboard flight. There was a sudden message from our number 3, who shouted "My guns have jammed! My guns have jammed!", which got the response "Keep formation, Jens, you might draw some of the enemy fire." Then we opened fire and, with the concentration of .303 bullets hitting near the Heinkel's wing root it just broke off, and two of the enemy crew were making vain attempts to bale out before the plane hit the sea. However, the fight wasn't over, and we broke left and circled round for another attack. As we did so their front gunners tried to get a bead on us, but as we came round, helped by the cloud cover, we were soon out of their range of view. This next time they were waiting for us, and thin red dots started drifting from their guns toward us. These were tracer bullets, which were added to the high explosive bullets in order to help the gunner's aim.

Another message: "Red 2, this is Red Leader. There's a bomber to port that is struggling. Go for it, and I'll cover your tail." I saw the struggling bomber and responded "Roger Red Leader. Tally ho!" This time I knew exactly what I was going to do. I had to weave a little to avoid the tracer from the Heinkel's top turret, but I closed the range to 200 yards or less before opening fire with a long burst, aiming for the engines. Once the engine was gone, the bomber would either have to drop its bombs or go straight down. In this case it was the latter. The enemy bomber attack had been a disaster. There were already other planes streaming smoke, or with damage elsewhere. In the end I think we destroyed five, but a couple of the others were so badly damaged that they may not have made it back. The French squadron that had been scrambled with us also claimed a couple of bombers destroyed.

There was something of a celebration that evening. We had faced the Luftwaffe, and struck them hard. Even I was credited with one and a half kills, which I had triumphantly painted below the cockpit of my Hurricane. The only pilots who weren't feeling so good were Jens Fredrikson, who wasn't able to get a shot off at the bombers after his guns jammed, and another pilot from Yellow flight, who stopped a few bullets in the wing of his Hurricane.

On 22nd August we received news that we would be transferred with the French squadron to 11 Group down south. They were taking heavy losses, and with some squadrons having to scramble several times each day they needed to withdraw to rest and regroup. Air Chief Marshal Dowding, who was in charge of 11 Group, did not appear to rate foreign fighter pilots very highly, so our French buddies were determined to go all out to prove him wrong. The weather had been poor, and fewer raids had been carried out. That gave us the opportunity to move to our base in the 11 Group Sector early on 24th August, which dawned bright and clear. The base looked like a lonely flying club airfield in a rural setting. Just like home! Because of the attacks on many of our airfields our fighters had been using some of the grass airstrips on the local flying club airfields. We were happy to manage with them, even if they were a bit bumpy.

We didn't have long to wait to be scrambled. The sector station called us on the phone at about 11 am on 26th August, saying there were 100+ bandits heading for the coast. We were soon airborne, and soon joined up with a Spitfire squadron based further south. After about 12 minutes we saw many bandits, the main formation made of He111 and Dornier Do17 bombers, but we also spotted enemy fighters above acting as the escort. The leader of the Spitfire squadron radioed to say that they would take on the Me109 fighters whilst our Hurricanes went for the bombers. This time it wasn't so easy, and we had to watch our tails all the time for any Me109s which broke through the Spitfire screen trying to protect us. If they did so then we had to break and turn, because the Hurricane could turn inside a Me109, if they tried to out-turn us. That gave us an advantage. The main problem we had to face was the cannon shells that were part of the Me109's armament. A single shell could cause heavy damage, whereas machine-gun bullets could cause some damage, but in most cases the plane would still be controllable. One of the pilots in Blue Flight forgot to look over his shoulder and was attacked by a Me109 from about four o'clock, which destroyed his rudder. All he could do was to turn the Hurricane on its back and bale out. The Home Guard picked him up on the ground and he was soon able to get back into action.

There was also news of an attack on London on the night of 24th August. We weren't sure whether it was intended or not, but Bethnal Green was certainly hit. We met a Bomber Command pilot back at base who had baled out of a Wellington bomber, and he told us that a squadron of Wellingtons had been sent to bomb Berlin as a sort of retaliation measure. I'm sure Hitler didn't like that one bit.

We were getting attacks day after day, and the Germans were showing no sign of letting up. There seemed to be more and more fighters flying in amongst the bomber formations, because at that speed they would use up more fuel and reduce their range still further. Their fighters only had enough fuel for 10 minutes' flying time over England. They must have been desperate to protect the bombers. However, we had to pay the price. One of the pilots in particular, Freddie Peterson, who was flying at number 3 in Yellow flight, was well known to some of the others for his gambling habits. He was a brave pilot, but always willing to spend a bob or two on the horses or greyhounds, which meant that we often had to give him a bit of extra financial support. Soon after Freddie went down in the Channel his parents came to see the Squadron Leader to collect his personal effects. The regular Chaplain was away, so because he knew I had had Pastoral experience, the Squadron Leader asked me to go with him to speak to Freddie's family. I told him that I would certainly do so, because there had been times in our village when families needed a touch of comfort, understanding and sympathy. I was able to tell Freddie's parents that I had been flying in the same squadron at the time of his death, and that the cockpit of his Hurricane had been absolutely shredded by the combination of cannon and machine-gun fire from a fighter which had suddenly bounced us. It was all so quick, and there was no way he could have escaped. His luck had just run out. They were pleased to know that he had shown such courage right up to the end. Having flown with Freddie, many of the other pilots would have said exactly the same. I was able to tell them that he had given his life not only for King and Country, but for all the Christian beliefs and justice that we held dear in our hearts. He would probably be remembered for much longer than those of us who survived.

It wasn't just us in 11 Group who were trying to bear the burden. We asked for help from 12 Group as well, but they always seemed to be late getting in on the fight. They had been trying a tactic that they called a 'Big Wing', which meant several squadrons of fighters coming in together, but they took far too long to assemble and reach the point of action, wherever that was. They seemed to think that it was more worthwhile destroying 20 bombers on the way back than one bomber before it reached its target. It was all so controversial.

CHAPTER 12

We had been struggling a little, with more and more enemy planes coming over every day, yet fewer and fewer replacement pilots. On average the ones that were sent to us only had nine or ten hours' flying time on a Hurricane, so they were very inexperienced. I understood that on 1st September so many planes came over in wave after wave that all the squadrons in 11 Group, including all the reserve squadrons, were airborne together.

I must admit, I spent one day off duty with my Bible in the chapel at the base. I started to read through the first letter written by the apostle Peter, and read "Cast all your anxiety on God because he cares for you." (1 Peter 5:7) If there was a time to pray, then this was it. The letter went on: "Be self-controlled and alert. Your enemy the devil prowls around like a roaring lion looking for someone to devour. Resist him, standing firm in the faith, because you know that your brothers throughout the world are undergoing the same kind of suffering." (1 Peter 5:8-9) That was true enough. Then finally "And the God of all grace, who called you to his eternal glory in Christ, after you have suffered a little while, will himself restore you and make you strong, firm and steadfast." (1 Peter 5:10) That was why we had to hold on now.

During the first week in September things became tough. Many pilots were reaching exhaustion point and others, including myself, were due leave that we just could not take under the circumstances. It was good not only to get letters from the family, but to have my Bible to read when I really needed some support. It was the one book I knew I could rely on.

Suddenly, on 15th September, everything seemed to change again. The Luftwaffe had started night-time attacks, as well as daylight raids, so we were getting used to acting as night fighters. On that day we were scrambled to intercept a formation of enemy bombers heading west and, as usual, we were given height and compass bearing. When we got to the interception point we had been given we found absolutely nothing, and no enemy aircraft were in sight. We later found that the bomber formation had changed course and was heading straight towards London. It came as a total surprise, and Ground Control had not expected this move.

London docks were hit quite badly, as well as many of the civilian areas. London was the biggest capital city in Europe, so they could hardly miss their targets once the incendiaries had started fires around the city. Talk about fire from above!

Our defences were even more limited around London due to the shortage of anti-aircraft guns in general, which forced us to have them deployed rather too thinly in some areas. We all thought this was a big mistake on the part of the Luftwaffe, because their raids up until then had been concentrated against RAF airfields, and the destruction they had wrought there had devastated our fighter defences. If they had stopped attacking the airfields, then maybe it would have given us the opportunity to regroup and build up our strength once again. Not only that, it would also bring the bombers within range of all the fighters from 12 Group. It must have been our retaliatory attack on Berlin that started it all. Maybe my recent prayers were to be answered after all!

During the rest of September, and most of October as well, the Luftwaffe made repeated night-time raids on London. They must have expected us to be drastically short of planes by that time, but we soon gave them a big surprise; one big raid was met by over 300 of our Hurricanes and Spitfires from both 11 and 12 Group airfields. But not everything has been easy. In one encounter our Flight Commander, Jimmy Whiteside, had to bale out of his burning Hurricane, and came down with severe burns to his face and hands. I went to the hospital yesterday to see him, and he was still able to give me a smile through all the bandages that were wrapped around him. He said to me "John, you're a strange man. You're a good pilot, and go all out to do your job, which is to down as many enemy aircraft and pilots that you can, and you will kill them if necessary. Yet you're not just a Christian believer, but a Pastor as well, and I always thought that they had a more pacifist attitude, to go out and offer life to the wicked. I just don't understand it!"

I replied that in the Bible there were times when God even destroyed those who fanatically worshipped idols. I said that the Germans saw Hitler as an idol. We were acting to uphold our Christian truths, whilst Hitler seemed to care for no one but himself. It was like the story of Elijah, who challenged the priests of Baal to prove that their idol even existed. Two bulls were to be cut up as sacrifices, but the wood underneath them was not to be ignited. Elijah said to the priests "You call on the name of your god, and I will call on the name of the Lord. The god who answers by fire - he is God." (1 Kings 18:24) The priests of Baal frantically shouted and danced round their altar all day, but there was no response. Elijah then built his own altar from stones, with the bull on top, and doused it several times with water. He then prayed to God to accept his sacrifice, and went on "Answer me, O Lord, answer me, so these people will know that you, O Lord, are God, and that you are turning their hearts back again." (1 Kings 18:37) God responded mightily to Elijah's prayer, and the people saw that they had been worshipping nothing but an idol. The priests of Baal were later put to death.

When I got back to base I found that I had been promoted to Flight Lieutenant, and would be leading B Flight. I also found that because of my score of confirmed kills, which had risen to five and a half, I would officially be recognized as a Fighter Ace, and I had been recommended for a Distinguished Flying Cross. Everything seemed to be happening at once, because our Squadron Leader, who had now been promoted to Wing Commander, told us that we were to be moved to a base in the 10 Group Sector, where another squadron would be posted to join us. I immediately sent Ruth a letter about my DFC, saying that as soon as we arrived at our new base we were to be allowed 72 hours' leave, so I would make my way to the village to meet her. That would be early in November.

It was so good to see Ruth safe when I got home on the Saturday. More foods had been rationed, so it was hard finding everything she needed for little Mary and Ruby in particular. Ruth was a very practical person, and had skills which she had probably learned from her father Edward as a child. These she was able to put to good use through the village, and she earned a bit extra by using her motherly skills at the country house where several young evacuees were living. She was also able to take Mary and Ruby to the home to play with the children there, something which they all enjoyed. The owner had some dairy cattle, which came in useful where the youngsters were concerned, and because of her valuable work there Ruth was often given a spare bottle of milk to take home for herself. When I saw Charles again all he could talk about was the best way to prepare rabbit stew. I think it had all rather gone to his head. There were plenty of other smaller, if quite original, ideas for meals or snacks. On Sunday it was also nice to visit the church for the morning service, where I was welcomed by all, including the Pastor. His face had become thinner, but it still had that regular big smile.

The Battle of Britain may have been won, but the war certainly was not over yet. Where most people used to go for a swim at the seaside, there were now thick rows of barbed wire, anti-tank defences, and usually mines laid along the beach. I heard of one person who inadvertently strayed into a minefield. His friend was saying that this person had always been a rather careless character, sometimes taking warnings with a pinch of salt. Sadly, he wouldn't need any salt where he ended up. Even fears of a German invasion were reducing now, especially since we had made bombing raids on all the many invasion barges the Germans had very kindly left waiting side by side in the French ports. Also, with the winter approaching, it would not be until next year that Hitler could expect the right weather along with the right tides to attempt any sort of invasion.

The Luftwaffe's main target was now London, but there was news of attacks taking place elsewhere. We thought we were relatively safe in the Midlands, but during November there had been devastating raids on Birmingham, Wolverhampton and Coventry. Even the old cathedral was destroyed in Coventry. These were not too far from home, so I wondered if Ruth and the family were taking any extra precautions. In the city each household had been issued with an Anderson shelter which had to be buried somewhere in the garden, stocked up with a few emergency rations and seating and covered with either sandbags or earth. It was a simple structure, but one that tended to suffer from the damp inside.

We pilots tended to have much more time on our hands than before. Instead of visiting the local pub near the base, the Rabbit Warren, for hours on end simply to get drunk, or visiting the improvised cinema in the village hall to watch films that had already been shown several times over, I tried to make time between missions to study French. My Free French tutor gave me plenty of practical experience in conversation. After a short while I felt it was becoming something of a second language to me, and I gained the admiration and respect of the French pilots for my efforts.

Meanwhile, we were getting some replacement pilots in to bring our squadrons up to full strength again. I asked one young pilot how many hours he had on a Hurricane. When he replied "Eight hours, sir" I promptly told him that we would go up together, make it nine hours, and that I would give him his first baptism of fire. Once airborne I tried the same trick that my old flying instructor had used on me, to dive on the new recruit with the "tac-a-tac-a-tac-a-tac-tac" of an imaginary machine-gun ringing through his ears over the radio! Later, because I had mentioned the baptism of fire, the fact that my name was John, and the fact that I had been a church Pastor, everyone, including the members of the other squadrons on the base, started calling me John the Baptist, a nickname which somehow stuck.

As we moved towards our second wartime Christmas there were those who considered that any Christmas celebrations or festivities should be replaced by more action in the factories. They claimed that one extra artillery shell made was worth more than 20 greetings cards sent. I'm sure opinion was divided, because I saw many venues prepared for entertainment. I sent little Mary a birthday card, together with a little doll that had been knitted by a member of the local Women's Institute. I would like to have been with them for Christmas, but duty came first. Even if the weather was bad and flying impossible, there was plenty to get on with.

We had been waiting eagerly for Christmas to come when the Wing Commander informed us quietly that he had received further orders, and our squadron was being posted elsewhere. On 28th December we must be ready to leave, but where for? During the time we had left we said our personal goodbyes to the pilots of the French squadron who had played a big part with us during the Battle of Britain. I had much to thank my French tutor for, and I promised him that I would continue my French language studies, as well as getting whatever practice I could with conversation.

On that day we saw a big transport aircraft parked on the runway and, at about 1100 hours, we boarded it for the trip to our new base. There were remarks about the tropical uniforms stashed in the rear of the Halifax, and we guessed that where we were going had to be somewhere relatively hot. Several hours later the plane landed on the main runway at Gibraltar, and we were taken to our barracks near the airfield.

The next day we met our new Squadron Leader, who said that his orders were to get us on board a certain cargo ship that would be docking in the next few days. That was all he was permitted to say at the time. As we had expected, several ships soon arrived in convoy. However, because of delays, the convoy didn't leave Gibraltar until 6th January 1941. Once safely on board the Squadron Leader informed us that we were on our way to Malta with fighter reinforcements. Since Benito Mussolini's declaration of war against Britain on 10th June 1940, in support of his Nazi ally, the small island of Malta had become a vital link in the Mediterranean. Because of the importance of the convoy, the carrier HMS *Illustrious* was to provide air cover, together with patrols to hunt for enemy submarines. The Italians didn't want to make things easy for us! The Fairey Fulmars on board the carrier might have had more success against the old CR42 biplane fighter escort that the Italians were still using, but the slightly underpowered planes couldn't prevent several Luftwaffe bombers scoring direct hits. It was fortunate that *Illustrious* had an armoured deck, which limited the damage caused, but there were still a number of casualties on board.

The ship limped into Malta with the rest of the convoy. Unloading was started immediately by the dock workers in Grand Harbour, Valetta, and repairs were begun on the damaged fleet carrier. There were 12 crated Hurricanes on board our ship, and these were soon on their way to Takali, the most central of the three RAF airfields on the island. Once at the airfield, the RAF mechanics would prepare the planes for service, distributing them amongst the various blast pens that had been built. They would soon be fuelled by hand with the precious 100 octane fuel and re-armed. The belts for the machine-guns had to be carefully prepared by hand, ensuring that armour-piercing and high explosive bullets were inserted in the correct order. This was an island fortress where every moment lost could mean that a Hurricane might not be ready to intercept the next air raid. Every time an alert was sounded, a red flag would be raised in the harbour area, warning people to take cover. Barracks were basic structures, a sergeant's mess on the edge of the airfield made of sandstone that looked like a large hollow block of stone. Even the Ground Control building looked like something out of the Stone Age. Remarks were even made about the sanitary facilities, particularly by men who waited outside the female lavatories and teased the WAAFs, because strict restrictions had been enforced on the use of toilet paper. The island's newspaper, *The Times of Malta*, was printed on very thin paper that usually acted as a good substitute!

Being a new squadron on the island, we were invited to the Governor's residence. The Governor, Lieutenant General Sir William Dobbie, was certainly a man to be admired. He had kept the population of Malta together ever since the beginning of the siege the previous year. He is one who has performed his duty in the defence of the island, but in many ways he has demonstrated the sincerity of his Christian beliefs in doing so. In the early days of the siege, the governor issued a Special Order of the Day that stated: "The decision of His Majesty's Government to fight on until our enemies are defeated will have been heard with the greatest satisfaction by all ranks of the garrison of Malta. It may be that hard times lie ahead of us, but however hard they may be, I know that the courage and determination of all ranks will not falter, and that with God's help we will maintain the security of this fortress. I therefore call upon all officers and other ranks humbly to seek God's help, and then, in reliance upon Him, to do their duty unflinchingly."

It wasn't long before we had our first taste of action, because raids on Malta were becoming more frequent. Bombers from both the Italian Regia Aeronautica and German Luftwaffe made their presence known daily. As the winter began to fade and the early dawn of spring approached, the raids even increased. Through the first two weeks of February 1941 there were twice as many raids as in the whole of January, and the raids continued into March, by which time the Luftwaffe was also sending Me109 fighters over the island. Life was hard, and the shelters that had been dug out of the rock many feet underground began to reek of sweat, condensation and mould, as well as suffering from the lack of toilet facilities. Malta, though only a small island, is one of the most densely populated areas in Europe. Many bunks were constructed within the big cave-like shelters for those whose homes had been destroyed in the bombing, of which there were many.

We had our successes, and my confirmed kills went up to nine, but if any aircraft came back damaged it might either be used for spare parts, or the engineers turned up with parts that they had made, though there were cases of items being "borrowed" from the dockyard. There were few means by which Malta could support itself, so the provisions supplied on a convoy that arrived at the end of March were gratefully received, even though restrictions were still tight.

By now I had been on the island for three months, and I had never before missed Ruth and Mary so much. I longed to see them, as well as the rest of the family. Postal services were minimal, and one could only write that one was well, active, and busy doing one's duty. Much of the rest was censored. Such letters were supposed to act as morale-boosters to everyone at home, but whether this was the case is questionable.

It wasn't until April that I heard from Ruth, and it came as a great relief. She even enclosed a photo of herself and Mary, who was now four years old. She told me about some of the raids she could see which must have been in the Birmingham area, where there were several aircraft factories. There were searchlight beams wandering through the sky, and she could see the flash of the anti-aircraft shells exploding here and there. There must have been quite a heavy raid during the night, because when everything had gone quiet again she could still see the red glow in the sky from the fires caused by the incendiary devices.

The one scare they had was when a stray bomber came over land owned by one of the neighbours and dropped a parachute mine. It must have had a faulty detonator, because it lay stuck in the field until the next morning when men from the Bomb Disposal Unit came along and successfully defused it. That must take real courage. They don't know what exactly happened to the bomber, but the wreckage of a Dornier was found some 20 miles to the west. If that was the same bomber, then it must really have been lost, because it was low on fuel yet still heading the wrong way. There were a couple of survivors who were badly shot up, but the rest of the crew probably died on impact.

Meanwhile, Jacob had received his call-up papers and had decided to join RAF Bomber Command. He had relatives in Shropshire, so he would be on familiar territory if he was lucky enough to be sent to the Training Unit in that area. His uncle had also been in the Great War, where he flew the big Handley Page 0/400 bombers, so I think he may have influenced Jacob's decision to join the RAF rather than enlist in the army or navy. My father's decision to suspend his air service, together with the fact that Jacob was often taken along as a co-pilot, may have influenced his decision. However, because of our farm, we applied for some Land Girls to take Jacob's place in helping Charles.

In Malta, we had a couple of recreational hobbies now that the sun is warmer. When off-duty a number of pilots and ground crew found a few beach areas below the cliffs where we could go swimming. The other activity, which I very much enjoyed, was an Officer's Christian Union, which had been in existence since last year. I was able to play an active role in this.

CHAPTER 13

Although we were playing our part against the enemy aircraft that came over, we desperately needed reinforcements. We were fortunate in that two groups of Hurricanes arrived at the beginning of May. They had been flown some 450 miles to Malta from the aircraft carrier HMS *Furious*. Things were now hotting up, and by the end of May we had received over 140 replacement Hurricanes. However, after the fall of Greece last March, the mood didn't exactly improve when we heard of the German invasion of Crete in May, where paratroops played a key part. By that time we had been on the island for about five months, and the atmosphere was really getting to us.

Rather than receive more fighter reinforcements, a squadron of Wellington bombers and the new Bristol

Beaufighter fighter-bombers were sent out with a view to attacking the ships that took Rommel's supplies from Sicily to North Africa. These were already being attacked by our submarines, but the more ships we could sink, the greater Rommel's need would be for supplies. Because of the bomber reinforcements that had arrived, we were flown out to Egypt, and arrived in Alexandria at the end of May. We thought at first that we would be getting a break, maybe even back in England, but it was not to be so.

One unusual thing did occur whilst I was in Alexandria. I was approached by the chief RAF Chaplain in the area, who had heard of my Pastoral experience, as well as involvement in the Officer's Christian Union in Malta. He told me of the opportunity for men like me to take a more active role not only to support those who were already Christians or churchgoers, but also to speak to those who, as yet, had no experience of Christianity, and the hope it gave them. I felt I had to consider this, but that I needed to pray about it. I was already an important part of our squadron, which did not have a regular Chaplain based with it, and I was one to whom other pilots could turn if they had any problems.

Rommel had been advancing steadily in North Africa with units of the Afrika Korps. Hitler had sent Rommel, whom he considered to be one of his top Generals, to support the Italian army after we routed them for the first part of 1941. A counter-attack was to be organized to stop the man whom we already knew as the Desert Fox, and we were to be a part of it. Yet this time we had a different role to play. We were to be equipped with the new Hurricane Mark 2 fighters, which were armed with four Hispano 40-millimetre cannon in the wings, and our task would be to destroy any Italian or German vehicles, including artillery, transport such as trucks or half-tracks, and maybe even tanks. The aircraft looked very oversized, having been fitted with the big Vokes filter underneath the engine to eliminate all the problems caused by the loose sand in the air. The sand was there all the time, and on a normal day we humans could usually put up with it. However, if we started flying at low level across the desert massive clouds of sand might appear.

Rommel's own tanks had much heavier armour than those used by the Italians, and would be much more difficult to destroy. However, if they were heavily damaged and, as we hoped, Rommel's supply of spares and fuel were limited, then we might even achieve our goal. At that time Tripoli was Rommel's only source of supply, and he had advanced with a view to taking Tobruk, an important deep-water port not too far from the Libyan/Egyptian border. Once again there were delays, and the main operation did not start until 10th June. It appeared that many of the tanks that had been involved in the battle were still either worn out or needed servicing.

On 7th June we took off on our first tank-busting mission. We knocked out plenty of vehicles with our concentrated cannon fire, which seemed to have some effect on the enemy troops, and when the main operation was put into action three days later everything seemed to be going according to plan, but heavy German resistance a week later forced us to retreat once again. Our thinly-armoured Matilda tanks just could not stand the fire from the enemy 88mm tank destroyers. Because of the concentration of infantry and the enemy fighter sweeps that were sometimes made against us, we decided to revert to our original Hurricane armament in the form of eight machine-guns. This would certainly prove more effective against infantry groups, and though cannons packed a big punch, we didn't consider the ammunition adequate to engage enemy fighters.

Then there was news of the sudden invasion of Russia in June. We wondered how Hitler could possibly have the troops to attack Russia, maintain a second front against us in Britain and also maintain the attacks by the Afrika Korps under General Rommel in North Africa. Had his lust for power made him blunder? Even so, right through until November, the battle in the desert ebbed and flowed. First we might advance, then we would find ourselves faced with superior enemy forces and be forced to fall back. The desert certainly wasn't a place for the faint-hearted. Even though we were fighter pilots with additional privileges to keep us going, in the open air we would have sand up our nose, in our eyes, and in our throats. The sand would blow across the dunes in clouds, and the thirst that the constant heat caused could be fatal.

After the failure of another operation in November, it was decided at last to put us on a plane back to England, where we would be given leave and posted to another base, possibly in 10 Group. This would be ideal for me because I would have good access to home. I hadn't seen the family for nearly a year and even though I had regular letters from everyone, nothing could replace the joy of being with them in person. The love and care you share in a partnership is something special, and to have an understanding family behind you is an inspiration.

When we eventually reached our new base in 10 Group I had to undergo a medical test. Not only had the last 12 months completely exhausted me, but I also needed to recover from the problems of food shortage in Malta and dehydration in the desert. I was told that I needed at least three weeks to recover fully. I was intent on getting home for Mary's birthday on 8th December, but frosty weather caused a shortage of passenger trains. I had to wait until 6th December. On the journey I could see the beauty of the white fields that were still glistening in the early morning sun. When I got off at the station I started to walk the two miles or so along the country lanes that led home, but after a short distance I saw old Bert coming along the road in his horse and cart. He was the local rag and bone man, and he would do anything for a spare copper, so I gave him a shilling to give me a lift, which he eagerly accepted.

One had to be a bit careful with Bert, because he was the sort who hardly knew the difference between recycling and looting. He told me of two men in smart trilby hats whom he'd met at the station a few weeks ago. They probably considered Bert easy prey, being a rag and bone man having to survive on what he could get and then sell on, and told him of a few "items" that they had obtained and wanted to sell on cheap. They said that when the air raid warning siren was sounded, many shopkeepers left their places of business immediately to head for the shelter. Some of them unfortunately left their front doors open. These men employed youngsters who would run in, collect whatever they could and leave quickly without being noticed. What they had collected would be passed on to the profiteers and sold on elsewhere.

But Bert wasn't as stupid as he might have appeared. When the train had left he took his horse and cart down to the police station and reported what he had been told. It may have caused little or no change in criminal activity, but at least Bert was honest enough to help the law.

Ruth spotted me coming down the road a couple of hundred yards away, and ran out to meet me. As I clambered down from the cart she put her arms round me and whispered "You're safe!" There had been so little news that she didn't even know that I was on my way back. For a moment I thought of King Solomon's description of the noble wife, whom he declares "is worth more than rubies. Her husband has full confidence in her and lacks nothing of value. She brings him good, not harm, all the days of her life. She selects wool and flax and works with eager hands. She is like the merchant ships, bringing her food from afar. She gets up while it is still dark; she provides food for her family and portions for her servant girls." (Proverbs 3:10-15) I felt there was so much more in the chapter that applied to Ruth, and I was so proud of her for the way she had dealt with our wartime crisis. She could almost be the perfect wife!

Mary and Ruby were spending a day with the other children at the country house, so we plotted to give them a big surprise when they returned. I hid behind the long blackout curtains when the children came home. Ruth led them into the living-room and announced that she had a surprise for them, and they looked puzzled. She then drew the curtain to reveal me standing there, and Mary's face just lit up with joy. She ran over to me shouting "Daddy!" and hugged me with her little arms, almost burying her head in my uniform. I lifted her up with a big smile and announced that I had to be there for her birthday. Ruby was pleased to see me as well. We didn't want to tell her yet of the heavy bombing that had taken place in Bristol, because her home had been in one of the main areas of the city that had been bombed, and we hadn't received any letters from her parents for a while. Alice had been out teaching at the school, so I didn't see her until later that afternoon.

The following day I decided to visit friends and family around the village; I had a few small gifts I had picked up whilst in Alexandria, where there were street traders everywhere. By coincidence the girls had recently been read the story of Aladdin and his magic lantern, and for the next few days they kept glancing over towards the lamp I had brought with me in case their own little genie came out.

I made sure my old Austin Seven was running and had enough petrol for me to reach the garage. The old Pastor was still in charge, and still smiling, so I told him about my meeting with the RAF Chaplain in Alexandria. He had a wonderful sixth sense, and at the time he had a feeling that something was up, that it wouldn't be long before the boot would be on the other foot, as the saying goes.

On the afternoon of 8th December we celebrated Mary's birthday with Ruby and a few of their friends, but we were careful to use our food rations as well as possible by making a few savoury snacks that Alice had seen in *Woman's Own* magazine, together with a small chocolate cake, though because of the sugar shortage we were unable to cover it with icing. We followed this with a strawberry jelly, which was very easy to make. Charles, being an experienced carpenter, even made Mary a wooden doll's house as a birthday gift. Ruby was just as excited at the time, because she had been lucky enough to have her request played by Uncle Mac on the children's radio show *Children's Hour*. They both listened to it regularly. My father still had a good sense of humour, so he was more likely to listen to Tommy Handley.

The following day it was as if the Pastor's thoughts had come true, because we were listening to the radio when we heard devastating news from America. On 7th December Japanese bomb and torpedo aircraft attacked the American Pacific Fleet docked and static in Pearl Harbor, Hawaii, and crippled the Pacific Fleet. For months President Roosevelt had been using all the means at his disposal to avoid a major confrontation. The terms for a political treaty had been sent to the Japanese government time and time again, but there had been little response. Japan's most recent military attacks had even forced Roosevelt to stop all supplies of oil to the country.

Early on the fateful morning a number of planes came in and headed for all the main battleships close together at anchor, whilst others headed for the airfields where the Americans had the majority of their planes parked side by side. Other random bombing took place against both civilian and military buildings, whilst fighters machine-gunned many of those fleeing or seeking shelter at the scene. In his speech to Congress the following day to demand that war be declared, Roosevelt said that 7th December was "a day that will live in infamy". It was later revealed that Japan had still been making peace negotiations with the Americans at the time of the attack, and it was not until some hours after the attack that officers from the Japanese Foreign Embassy delivered an official Declaration of War to the American government.

The Americans had been supplying us through a Lend/Lease Agreement signed by both Churchill and Roosevelt, but now they had a military role to play. Hitler had declared war on America as well, in support of his allies in the Axis Pact, so America was now really in this war with us.

Just over two weeks later the whole family attended the Christmas Day service at the church. After an introductory carol the Pastor invited me to the front, where thanks were given and prayers offered for my safety. He even said that he had been given a sign that God would use me in a far greater way than I imagined, but at the time his words puzzled me. I couldn't quite understand what he meant.

CHAPTER 14

By the second weeks in January I was certainly feeling healthier. I had put on weight and felt much better in general, so I contacted the CO at our base in 10 Group and requested that I be returned to duty. My request was granted, but combat was certainly limited, and tended to be more at night. It wasn't until February that we had any action other than the occasional routine patrols.

Then one night at about 2200 hours we had a telephone call again, whilst some of us were hanging around the sheds near the airstrip. We glanced over, expecting it to be another routine patrol duty, but the officer inside shouted "Scramble!" We rushed to our parked Hurricanes and quickly carried out all the pre-flight checks we knew so well. A green Very light wafted into the air as a take-off signal, and I indicated to my flight that we should taxi onto the runway. We saw another flight lifting off the ground in front of us, so I gave the signal "Full throttle. Let's go!" As we took off the landing lights on the runway showed their brightness for a fraction of a second as we passed them, but we were soon airborne and away.

Ground Control soon indicated that enemy aircraft were heading in a north-westerly direction, probably to carry out another raid on the aircraft factories in Bristol. They also gave us the usual range, height, and directions for us to intercept. At first it was hard to see the aircraft because enemy bombers on night attacks had all been painted black. However, the flight ahead of us spotted them and identified them as long range Junkers Ju88 bombers, escorted by Messerschmitt Bf110 'Zerstörer' twin-engined fighter-bombers. They were heavily armed, with four cannon in the nose and a single machine-gun operated by the rear gunner, but they certainly lacked the manoeuvrability of the single-engined Me109. There were no Spitfires with us, so a squadron that had just joined us was ordered to take on the Me110s and give the rest of us some extra air cover.

By this time I felt the Germans were likely to have new pilots on the job, as we must have downed so many of their experienced pilots since the war began, and other pilots were being used on the Russian front. For once, I was right. The Junkers bombers had long-range fuel tanks, and the moment we hit them they went up in smoke with the aircraft. Altogether we downed about eight Ju88s, and the squadron above us did well against the Bf110s, scoring five confirmed kills and a couple of probables. Even I added to my score.

However, having done at least two full tours of duty, and because of my borderline health situation, I was offered a post with an Operational Training Unit. I wasn't sure whether to take it. Eventually I agreed, a little reluctantly, and was posted to an OTU in the west of England. Imagine my surprise when I walked into the CO's office only to find that it was my old Flight Commander, Jimmy Whiteside. Once the formal reception duties had been carried out, Jimmy invited me along for an informal chat to catch up on all our experiences. He still showed signs of his burns, and he had grown a big handlebar moustache to cover a few of the remaining scars. He explained that his healing process had taken much longer than expected, and he had undergone several operations in the hospital. When he came out the RAF weren't sure whether to put him back on combat duties or post him elsewhere, where they considered he could be of most use. They knew of his disciplined attitude toward flying, so they put him in charge of the OTU there. He added that in the end he had found that it wasn't too bad after all. I shared my experiences with him, adding that I had now gained 11 confirmed kills. He smiled as he looked over towards me and said "I knew you could do it, from the moment you joined my flight!" Coming from him, that was a real compliment.

However, in the early months of 1942 the war was not going too well for us. As the Japanese attacks continued in the Pacific there was news that the giant fortress of Singapore had surrendered, whilst in North Africa the promoted Field Marshal Rommel was advancing as well. The one piece of good news we received was that the island of Malta, where I had been posted for the first half of 1941, had been awarded the George Cross by King George VI. The award citation ran: "To honour her brave people I award the George Cross to the Island Fortress of Malta, to bear witness to a heroism and a devotion that will long be famous in history". It was said to be the most bombed place on earth, which I could quite believe, and the siege was not over yet. The courage of all the Maltese civilians on the island, and those who had joined His Majesty's forces as anti-aircraft gunners, mechanics, or merely labourers, to name but a few, is quite exceptional.

The OTU wasn't just a place for theory, but for practical application of it. I spoke to the CO, who, in times like this, always told me to relax and call him Jimmy. During the Battle of Britain we had both noticed that the enemy fighters kept a different formation from us. We had always used a V-shaped formation made up of three planes, but there had been complaints from the pilots in my squadron that they spent endless time looking to keep tight formation next to their Flight Commander. This gave them little time to actually look around for the enemy, and they were sure it was one reason why new pilots were more likely to get shot down. The Luftwaffe pilots used a more open formation called a *schwarme*, made up of four planes. It looked rather like the position of one's fingers, and each plane was able to cover the tail of the one ahead of it. He agreed right away, and we made a few trial runs with pilots who already had two or more hours in a Hurricane. It turned out to be a great success. We found we had more time to look around, and the formation, being more open, was easier to break from in case of trouble and easier to reform once ordered. I understand he wrote to the Air Chief Marshal in charge of 10 Group explaining the proposed formation changes.

At Easter I was given 48 hours' leave to visit the family. It wasn't a long time, but to be with one's family for a short time can be so much more encouraging than not at all. This time I was able to telephone Ruth and tell her what time I would arrive at the railway station. All around the big railyards and sidings there were signs of military hardware. Since America had joined the war, much more American hardware had been turning up, and one only had to look for a moment to see wagons loaded with tanks and under heavy tarpaulins, or stocks of their regular general purpose car, which they called the Jeep. On another side might be stocks of artillery and shells, many of which were covered over with camouflage netting.

Ruth was waiting at the station with my Austin Seven, which now had hooded headlights. She told me she had been taking driving lessons, but still needed someone to accompany her, as she didn't yet have a full driving licence. Ruth's friend Sarah Williams was the landlord of the Dragon, the local inn, which was near the station. This made it quite easy for her to accompany Ruth on the way to the station, then make her own way to the Dragon and let me accompany Ruth for the short journey back. It was a shame that the traditional idea of presenting an Easter egg had been curtailed, simply because of all the food shortages. By this time eggs were rationed to one or two per week, and much of the real food was being replaced with powdered substitutes, so other ideas had to be found. Ruby suggested that we could melt a chocolate bar into a small mould, which would have been a good idea if we had been able to find a suitably small egg-shaped mould.

Meanwhile I asked my father what his opinion was of the new RAF flight formation we had considered. He said that in his day aircraft had been much slower and much easier to keep in formation, so a revised formation for our fast monoplane fighters would not go amiss. The following day was Easter Sunday, so we went to the church for the morning service. After this the Pastor called me over and asked if I remembered what he had said after the Christmas Service, about reaching out. My curiosity was aroused immediately, and after my positive response he invited myself and Ruth into the back room that he used as an office.

The Pastor told me he knew of a group with the initials SACA, which stood for the Soldiers' and Airmen's Christian Association. I remembered that the RAF Chaplain in Alexandria had mentioned being a reader, and wondered if this could have any connection. He explained to me that the amalgamation in 1938 of The Army Scripture Readers and Soldiers' Friends Society with The Soldiers' and Airmen's Christian Association had allowed Christians serving in the forces to witness to others in a much more open way. The members of the Association were not official chaplains but men who, through their contact with servicemen, might act as the spark that brought a man to believe in Christ, and then encourage new Christians in their faith and works. It also meant I would be able to become a Reader if I so desired, but still be able to fly, which seemed to be an ideal solution.

The Pastor had made a few enquiries of his own through Bishop Michael, with whom he was in regular contact, and he had been given the name of an RAF Chaplain at our OTU base whom I might wish to contact once I returned to duty. It was strange how the Pastor had the ability to almost read one's mind. He seemed to know exactly what I might wish to do.

I had met the Chaplain back at base, and he very kindly gave me an introduction to a Scripture Reader's duties. They were, he said, to spread the word of God, to strengthen all who already had a knowledge of the Christian faith, and to bring others to believe in Jesus Christ. At first I suppose I considered it a method of military evangelism. The Chaplain added that it might involve anything from Gospel services, starting prayer meetings or prayer groups, and Bible studies, to mission work, all of which I had already had experience in whilst acting in the village church.

For the next few days I had to pray specifically about all this, because there were mutterings from those who had no religious beliefs to speak of that I was just joining the church to get a more comfortable life preaching! When I next saw the Chaplain I felt sure that this was the right thing to do. I said that God had given me a word from the Bible, which was about the Philippian jailor who asked Paul and Silas "Sirs, what must I do to be saved?" (Acts 16:30) I told the Chaplain that there must be so many like that jailer, wanting to know about God, yet not knowing how to do it. Acting as a Scripture Reader would be my way of opening doors.

To my request to apply for membership as a Scripture Reader, the Chaplain told me that there were three main qualifications. These were (a) a genuine conversion to Christ (b) evidence of a new life in Christ (c) a desire to witness for Christ. I shared certain events that had happened in my life, and also said that both my Bible college Principal and our village Pastor, whom he knew well, could give me good references. Eventually my application was approved. I appreciated that the Chaplain was still in charge, but he would be able to give me a few hints about my new life and duties as a Scripture Reader.

At the western end of the base stood a large wooden building that had been used to house wounded men sent back to England from the front line during the Great War. This building was now disused, but I felt it offered a real opportunity to use it for God's work and to spread the Gospel message. It had one large room that had originally been used to treat the wounded, but I saw that it could be the ideal place to use as a room for prayer or Scripture meetings. There was also a smaller room at one end that a matron or doctor might have used as an office, together with a small kitchen that we could use for our regular cups of tea and any other available refreshments. Naturally, there had to be suitable sanitary facilities as well.

The layout was ideal, but the rooms were thick with dust and needed furnishing. A few of the WAAFs very kindly offered to do the cleaning inside, which they did very industriously over the next week. The Chaplain took on his shoulders the problem of furniture, and had the idea that where the bombing had been heaviest there were no doubt families who had not survived, and their furniture may have been picked up by the scrap dealers who always roamed the streets seeking to make money. He made a few enquiries, and when the room was ready we had a large sofa and three armchairs delivered, as well as a number of wooden chairs and a small table. He had applied for, and actually received, some funding towards all this, but we and several of the officers on the base agreed to share any payments over the total of the funding. But God was providing for us in a mighty way, and Mollie Layton, landlord of the King's Head public house near the base, offered us an old piano for use in services. She declared that she had bought a new piano just before the war, but no one wanted the old one, so she had simply kept it in storage behind the pub. It had a few wandering notes, and the cover on the back needed replacing, but a good piano tuner could fix that in no time at all.

Even though there was still much happening in the war, and Bomber Command was beginning to make a real contribution. In February a new Commander, Air Marshal Sir Arthur Harris, had been appointed, and in a warlike speech that echoed a biblical text he declared "They sowed the wind, and now they are going to reap the whirlwind." He favoured area bombing, rather than strategic bombing, claiming that instead of merely attacking a small yet specific target, regardless of its importance, the area bombing could bring the enemy to its knees by lowering their morale with destruction over a wide area.

In May he ordered all available bombers to attack the city of Cologne. I understand over 1,000 bombers, taken from both Regular and Reserve Units, took part. Even though the raid was carried out at night, it had no fighter escort, and we suspected that the Germans would soon have new ways of detecting our bombers earlier, thus enabling them to get their fighters airborne against us.

Soon after that, at the beginning of June, the Americans struck the Japanese fleet a big blow when dive-bombers and torpedo planes from the carriers *Enterprise, Hornet* and *Yorktown* sank four Japanese fleet carriers during their assault on Midway. Had the Japanese taken Midway, it would no doubt have been used as a base from which the west coast of America could be attacked.

I had now been at the OTU for four months. We had spent much time in the air with the new pilots, teaching them about formations and combat flying and telling them a few of the tricks we had learned through our experiences. Some had moved on to other duties, others went as replacements to fighter squadrons, and there were some who accepted the invitation to try the new plywood aircraft, the De Havilland Mosquito. When we told them it was made of plywood they thought we were referring to a toy, but once they tried piloting the new two-seater aircraft they found its speed outstripped that of any existing fighters, and could be used to escape the enemy. Both Jimmy and I tried the fighter version of the plane, powered by two Merlin engines, and found it both very fast and very manoeuvrable. It was a plane that either of us would be comfortable in.

Most strategic bombing raids were being carried out by the United States 8th Air Force, both in occupied areas and in Germany itself. These raids were carried out in daylight, which meant that their bombing accuracy was increased, but they were also more susceptible to fighter attack in daylight. At first they believed that the box formations, as well as the high level that their B17 Flying Fortresses flew in, was almost impenetrable, but they were soon to discover otherwise. For this reason they had decided to use fighter escorts, provided by either the RAF or the USAAF. The only problem was that the range of our existing fighters, even with long-range fuel tanks, was not enough to escort the bombers all the way to the target and back.

One day Jimmy called me to his office and said, "The Yanks are screaming out for more escorts. Would you be willing to go? I've had orders to select a few pilots with combat experience and you were my first choice. You don't have to take the posting, but I can arrange it if you do. There's an extra stripe on your sleeve if you want it and, oh, and the planes are Mustangs."

I had certainly heard of the P-51 Mustang fighters and was excited at the thought of flying one. They had been delivered to the RAF earlier in the year, and were an American design aircraft with an Allison engine that gave them a speed of over 385 mph. They could also be fitted with long-range fuel tanks that would prove ideal for escort duties. I told Jimmy I would accept the posting right away. As for promotion, I told Jimmy that as a mere Flight Lieutenant I was able to mix freely with the men. As a Squadron Leader, and as he himself knew all too well, I would be set on my own and seen as their leader. Being a Scripture Reader as well, I didn't think I could manage being placed in that position, unless it was an official order. In exchange for the posting he smiled and told me he would give me the extra 48 hours, leave to tell everyone at home that I had a new posting, and to make sure I had everything I needed.

Back at home after an uneventful but rather uncomfortable and bumpy bus journey I revealed that the posting would probably be at an airfield in 12 Group. This was where many of the escort missions were controlled from. I also shared with Ruth a feeling of uneasiness deep down. I sensed that there was another, perhaps more specific reason, why Jimmy had offered me the posting. I couldn't work it out. Yes, I was one of the most experienced pilots, and I had seen plenty of combat, but there were others, so why had I been selected in particular?

Ruth was very comforting, and remarked that I had probably been offered the posting because, in her mind, they only wanted the best. She was sure that everything would work out safely and, when the time came, she, Mary, and even little Ruby sent me on my way with a little kiss.

Soon after I got back to base I was asked to go along to the Recreation Room and asked if I could deal with the disturbance inside. There was certainly some sort of noise going on, so I walked inside, only to be greeted by the cheers of many of the pilots in the OTU, to many of which I had for all this time been busy teaching my combat tactics. Even they didn't want to let me go without a big send-off, and I felt humble, yet very privileged. To those who had helped in the scriptural work, either by helping to distribute a few Bibles, or by merely offering their Christian support, I added that I would remember them in my prayers. In some ways I felt sad at having to leave them so suddenly, particularly because the Chaplain and I had shared the task of both leading many of these men to God, and also helping them to grow in the Spirit. But I thought of the apostle Paul, who had visited so many places on his journeys, yet never stayed too long in one place. Perhaps that was what God wanted to do with me.

When I reached my new base I reported to the CO, Wing Commander Jacques Reynard. He was a man with a limp caused by injuries that occurred when an anti-aircraft shell exploded a short distance underneath his Spitfire, scattering shrapnel through the air and into his cockpit. He still had fragments of the shrapnel left in his foot, because it had gone too deep to be removed safely. Because of the similarity of his own name to the French word for 'fox', he was always referred to as "Foxy", and he certainly applied his cunning on escort missions. I was to be a part of the French-Canadian squadron on the base, and the Wing was made up of two British squadrons, one of which also had Mustangs, one of which had long-range Spitfires, and our squadron with the Mustangs. The Canadians had come over on an American troopship early last year, and a number of them claimed to have been violently sick on the way over.

The Squadron Leader, Yves Chevalier, had a great sense of humour. His name was the same as the French word for 'horseman', so before a mission he would climb into his aircraft with a jockey's cap on. He said it suited him, particularly as he was now dealing with a Mustang!

The squadron had been hit hard over the last few weeks. On the last raid they said that the German radar chain had detected them and the approaching bombers far sooner than had been anticipated, and they had been hit by a hail of anti-aircraft fire first, and then had to deal with oncoming waves of enemy fighters. Everything had been too much for them, and they were in quite low spirits.

As I walked over toward the barracks I was welcomed by one of the other Flight Commanders, who took me to meet the rest of the squadron. There were those who made attempts to stand to attention, and others who sat muttering in French on the wooden chairs nearby. I suddenly realized that Jimmy must have sent me here because of my skills with the French language. However, some of them looked upon me as if I were just another replacement pilot. Because of this I asked the Squadron Leader, and the Wing Commander as well, if they would allow me to take a Mustang up and show the men some of the skills I really had. It might not only help them to accept me more for my flying, but it might just lift their spirits a little. It was an unusual request, but both officers could see my motives, so they cautiously agreed.

The next day, which was a sunny August day, I climbed aboard my Mustang with both officers and squadron pilots watching. The big Mustang needed some gentle handling, but I was able to perform some of the aerobatic manoeuvres I had sometimes used over in combat over the last two years, together with an unexpected one that had a real effect upon the men. A high-speed approach and pass over the airstrip at about 100 feet seemed to have them thinking, even if it did make the Squadron Leader duck!

As I taxied back off the runway towards the hangar and the waiting ground crew, the pilots already looked more cheerful, and as I climbed out of the Mustang onto the ground the Wing Commander approached me and commented "On any other occasion I would have you severely reprimanded for what you did up there. But you did it with my permission and I think you certainly lifted the men's spirits."

That is exactly what happened, and there were times when their curiosity was aroused in my personal life. I told them of my family, my friends, and also of my Christian beliefs, which I would be willing to share at any time. Because of their backgrounds, some of the pilots were Catholics, others Protestants, but I stressed that I was not there to preach a religion, but to preach Christ, whom I believed to be my Lord and Saviour.

CHAPTER 15

Our first mission together was as escort to a Dutch squadron that was leading a raid on one of the coastal ports in northern Germany. We had been given an assembly point, and ground crew had fitted the usual drop-tanks to our planes, which we would jettison once the enemy fighters approached. We also stayed well above and ahead of the bombers so we would have the advantage of speed if we had to dive on the fighters. It was a complete success, and a major part of the port was left in ruins. The bombers had hit the docks, as well as the nearby synthetic oil refinery, and there was smoke everywhere. We had engaged a group of Me109 fighters, but the new Fw190s that came in the second wave were much harder to fix one's sights upon, so we sent a message over the radio to the other squadron with the Spitfire Mark 9s that were just above us, and which could certainly match them.

The following Saturday one of the pilots approached me cautiously to say that on the ground he almost had a fear of death, but once airborne that fear lessened, yet it was still there. What could he do about? Initially I told him that anyone who didn't say they were afraid had to be lying. Our lives were in God's hands, not our own. Some of Christ's best-known apostles, like Peter and James, had to suffer harsh deaths because they believed in the Lord Jesus Christ and openly proclaimed his teaching. Men were fighting this war because they believed in democratic and Christian values. I couldn't tell him that everyone would survive, because that would not be true, but God holds dear all those who have fought and died in his name. I opened the small Bible I always kept in my top pocket and read "No king is saved by the size of his army; no warrior escapes by his great strength. A horse is a vain hope for deliverance; despite all its great strength it cannot save. But the eyes of the Lord are on those who fear him, on those whose hope is in his unfailing love, to deliver them from death and keep them alive in famine. We wait in hope for the Lord; he is our help and our shield. In him our hearts rejoice, for we trust in his holy name." (Psalm 33:16-21) If we believed in God, and put our hope in him, then he would be there to help us fight our battles. I believe this comforted him, because he had seen fellow pilots die in the air.

At Ruth's next birthday that August I had no leave due, so I sent a card instead. She was pleased to get it in time, and replied that she wanted to see me again. We both knew that even though we thought about each other every day, the endless periods of waiting were sometimes hard to endure. When I did see her she told me the story of Bill Campbell, who had joined the Home Guard in his latter years. His mind tended to waver, and during an exercise it caused a real problem, after he unfortunately lobbed a grenade through the window of an approaching van. He didn't realize that it was the plumber's van out on a delivery, and not the scrap vehicle that was the real target. Fortunately he forgot to pull the pin on the Mills bomb, and it simply clattered around inside the van for a few moments. The plumber, who had jumped to safety in absolute terror, was furious!

This was at the end of October, when the news that was circulating was that General Montgomery had stopped Rommel in his tracks at the small railway junction of El Alamein in North Africa. The large port of Tobruk had surrendered to the Afrika Korps in June, so to stop the enemy before they reached the Suez Canal in Egypt was of primary importance. Our agents had done a good job in misleading Rommel where our main positions were, then forcing him to attempt an attack where we were able to tie him down and then counterattack ourselves. Our aircraft in the area were apparently doing a good job as Rommel began to retreat.

A few days later, on 8th November, an Allied force made up of British and American troops invaded Africa east of Algiers. That put the entire Afrika Korps in a pincer grip from which they could not escape, because Rommel must have been very short on supplies, particularly water for his troops and fuel for the tanks, which must have guzzled it up.

Over the winter of 1942 our escort duties became fewer, due mainly to very cold weather. We knew some bomber raids were taking place, because we sometimes saw a large number of bombers going over. They really had to watch out for any icing on the wings, because unless dealt with it tended to go deeper and affect the control cables. At the end of December there were cold winds, heavy snow, then more rain and fog. Even though there were a few regular patrols, air activity was very restricted.

At the beginning of December the Wing Commander invited Ruth and the children to the base, and when I told him it was Mary's birthday on 8th December he put on a little treat for her. Later that day Ruth and I spent a pleasant evening at the dance, where the music was played by an RAF band, who accompanied songs sung by two attractive girls from ENSA. Ruby and Mary were asleep by the time it all ended, but a couple of WAAFs had offered to take care of them. They told me they had children of their own, so they could certainly look after ours. They stayed in the Wing Commander's quarters overnight, and the next morning the Squadron Leader and I took them to the station to wait for the train.

This was our fourth wartime Christmas, and we were having to make everything last longer. Any damaged clothes were usually repaired and re-worn. The Government had even issued advice on how to preserve coal! I wished they would come to our village so that Ruth can show them what it was really like to have two children shivering at night in the cold weather, however well they were wrapped up. Meat shortages were so common that at Christmas, an alternative was provided for the traditional goose meal. It was completely meat-free, and ironically called Mock Goose.

Because much of his work was now outside, my father caught a chill in the recent poor weather, and has had to stay at home in bed for a few days, with Maria faithfully looking after him.

Once the weather cleared, both sides resumed their bomber raids. Mid-way through January the raid we talked about most was one by the Luftwaffe on Canterbury. We caused them some losses, and feared that the iconic Canterbury Cathedral may have been hit, but our fears were relieved when we heard that the town itself had received some damage, but the cathedral was untouched.

On 13th February, which was a nice sunny day, we escorted a large group of heavy bombers to their attack on Wilhelmshaven. This was a night mission, and once again we met stiff resistance from the German defences. Our squadron was lucky, because most of it was anti-aircraft fire, but one Spitfire received a direct hit on his wing, which shattered with the impact of the high explosive shell. Fortunately the pilot managed to bale out. The enemy night fighters, a number of which were converted Bf110s, were using radar not only to zero in on the bomber stream, but also to avoid us.

At the beginning of March, after we had carried out a number of raids, during which we had a number of successes against the German night-fighters, it was decided that our experience was worthy of a more worthwhile role, so we were moved again. We soon discovered that enemy bombers were still pounding British civilian areas in towns and cities. Because of our experience, we were moved to an airfield in the south-west, so we could intercept these more sporadic enemy raids. We would still need to take care because we knew that new improved fighters were emerging. I understood that our squadron would also be receiving Spitfire Mark 9s.

On 7th March we were on duty when the telephone rang, and we knew right away what that meant - there was a raid on the way. In fact the enemy attacks in the south-east that day were rather scattered, but Ground Control gave us the necessary information to intercept the enemy. The Luftwaffe were still using their Heinkel and Dornier bombers in the same old way, so we gained height until the call went out "Bombers, looks like 20+, three o'clock low."

The Squadron Leader ordered us into line astern formation and then, one by one, we peeled off to starboard to attack. The accompanying squadron went high to watch for any prowling enemy fighters in the cloud. On the first pass we only damaged a couple of planes, so Philippe, pilot of O-Orange, turned round to attack the Dorniers head-on, hoping that the threat might cause them to break formation, which it did. The bombers completely lost formation, allowing us to attack them once again, but most of the Dorniers ditched their bombs over the Kent countryside and turned tail. However there were a couple of Do217s that strayed off course, and we hit them hard with our cannon. They were later confirmed as kills by the Home Guard units in the area.

By April we could all see that the war really was turning in our favour. The campaign in North Africa was coming to an end, the Russians had defeated the Germans heavily at Stalingrad and were advancing themselves, and even some of the Italian prisoners who were acting under guard as farm workers said they wanted Mussolini out. They felt he had betrayed them, and wanted to make peace possible, once their King had been restored to the throne. We still had to intercept the usual raids by the Luftwaffe, but far fewer aircraft were involved. Some days there were been high-speed raids carried out by bomb-loaded fighters, but their effect was minimal. On 13th April the Luftwaffe claimed to have bombed Bristol heavily again, but we understood that their direction-finding aids had sent them to Weston-super-Mare instead. The newspapers reported that a number of their unexploded bombs were found to be full of sand, and one even had a Union Jack in it!

Unfortunately even we had losses. At the beginning of May we were scrambled to intercept a raid heading north-east, possibly towards a target in the Midlands. We had become a skilled night fighter unit by now, and we once again met the bombers head on to break up their formation. My wingman, Anton Lovens, was a brave Canadian who was a bit of a loner, and when the message came through that enemy fighters had pierced the air cover and were coming down towards us he broke off his attack against the bombers and headed towards the Me109 fighters that were coming into view. I think he must have been looking for the glow from the engine exhausts. As he swirled round in the subsequent dogfight, there was a sudden call over the radio "Blue 2, you've got a 109 on your tail. BREAK, BREAK!" There was a sudden glow as his plane caught fire and started a slow descent towards the ground. "Blue 2, are you OK? GET OUT, Blue2!" But there was no answer. His radio had gone silent, and after a long, gruesome descent there was nothing but a massive explosion as his plane hit the ground.

We missed Anton. He had not only been a good pilot, if a little eager, but he was one of the regulars at our Bible classes. He had come to believe in Jesus Christ during his time on this squadron, and had come a long way since then.

We had always been provided with a quantity of suitable leaflets and tracts, but Anton was one of those who had asked me for a Bible. He had always read one regularly back home in Canada, and he told me that one of his favourite passages was "The eternal God is thy refuge, and underneath are the everlasting arms, and he shall thrust out the enemy from before thee and shall say 'Destroy them'." (Deuteronomy 33:27) I was even considering inviting him to take the next meeting with me. He knew what we were facing as we took on each mission, and his faith always brought him to say that he knew what would happen to his soul if he didn't come back from a mission.

Anton was still young and single, though he had made a special friend of the grocer's daughter in the town. I went to see her yesterday to give her the bad news. I hadn't expected to find that she was a Christian too, and had done much in the way of charity to demonstrate it. She was sad to hear of Anton's death, but she believed that Anton had maybe had a premonition that something might happen. Had this been the case, then we wondered if he courageously, if a little recklessly, went for the fighters alone in order to give us time to break off our attack on the bombers and reform against the fighters. He had given his life for those of his friends.

The following month we had even more good news from the front. First of all we heard that the Italians had pulled out of Albania, one of the first countries Mussolini had occupied as part of the new Italian Empire. Then, a few weeks later, on 10th July, Allied troops invaded Sicily. It wouldn't be long before Italy felt the full force of the Allied troops. Those Italian prisoners were certainly right about the mood in the country. Everyone knew the war was lost, and the majority wanted peace at any price.

The Luftwaffe was still making raids on the English Channel ports. We were up again at the end of July when enemy bombers were reported, but some of these were simply hit-and-run efforts, even if they were on quite a large scale. The anti-aircraft batteries were getting to them first, and by the time we had reached the intercept point the raiders had turned tail, sometimes with heavy losses. One of our Spitfires was even mistaken for an enemy fighter in the shadows of the evening, and returned with some damage to tail and wings. The Wing Commander telephoned the anti-aircraft control unit and gave them a real talking-to. He also reprimanded the pilot, who later admitted that he had not switched on the Identification Friend or Foe (IFF) transmitter in his cockpit.

By August, we were all celebrating Italy's request for an armistice. However, the Germans were clearly not giving up easily, because their forces had withdrawn to the north, presumably to make a stand. I had other things to celebrate. First of all, because of my long tour of duty, I was given 48 hours' leave to get back home for Ruth's birthday. The Squadron Leader also put all the Flight Commanders' names down for decorations. The Flight Commanders from 'B' and 'C' flights were awarded the Distinguished Flying Cross, and I received a Distinguished Service Order. I was told that it had been awarded "for courageous flying in the face of the enemy, and for all the work that has been undertaken to lift the pilot's morale and give them new hope." I knew I now had 15 confirmed kills against the enemy, but if it was anything to do with me trying to spread God's word as well then I was very privileged.

When I got back home the first thing I did was to give Ruth a tasty present, which was a big bag of apples that the Wing Commander had given me. I suppose I saw it as a belated birthday present. He had two apple trees outside his home near the base, so his wife and son were never wanting, and the cooking apples on one of the trees were ideal for some of the recipes that had been published since rationing began. Little Mary, who was well into her fifth year, was now beginning to grow up and act as a growing child, rather than as an infant. She would strut about the room in her little spotted dress just to show how quickly she was growing. Ruby was also doing well. She was nine years old and I wondered if she would become a teacher of sorts herself one day, because she was always curious about how things were done. She was born in the city, so rural life had been a new experience for her.

Ruby was doing well at school, and the personal contact they had with each other was a great help if Mary got stuck on a homework question. My father was keeping on with the farm, but because of the food shortage he had had to change his ways. All his beef cattle had gone and he now had two dairy cows, which needed to be milked every day. This was quite an exhausting job, but he still had the two land girls with him to help with the milking. His potato field had grown in size as well. However, I suggested that he should modernise his milking methods.

Another reason he changed was that he felt the children would do better with a good supply of milk, as well as the meat from the rabbits. Someone in the village suggested that he should try making either cheese or yoghurt, because cheese in particular was in very short supply, with three ounces the ration for a full week. The problem was, of course, that in a war with so many restrictions it was very difficult to find the necessary goods to replace what we had lost. The gentleman at the country house helped by providing some milk churns, which needed cleaning before they could be used.

On Sunday 19th September, we all managed to attend the morning service at the church, where the Pastor gave a good sermon about us being more than conquerors. He used the Scripture text that runs "Who shall separate us from the love of Christ? Shall tribulation or distress, or persecution, or famine, or nakedness, or peril or sword? As it is written: 'For thy sake we are killed all the day long, we are accounted as sheep for the slaughter.' Nay, in all these things we are more than conquerors through him who loved us. For I am persuaded that neither death, nor life, nor angels, nor principalities, nor powers, nor things present, nor things to come, nor height, nor depth, nor any other creations, shall be able to separate us from the love of God, which is in Christ Jesus our Lord." (Romans 8:35-39) I think he was trying to echo the forceful British spirit which had held up through all the bombing raids that Hitler and his Luftwaffe aces had made upon this country.

After the service I spoke to the Pastor, who was eager to hear what I'd been doing. I told him of the progress I'd made as a Scripture Reader, though there were often times when understanding or comforting words were needed, especially if I had to speak to the families of pilots who had been shot down or posted as missing. There were occasions when that grief was tempered by news provided by the enemy giving the names of those who had been taken prisoner, but it would always be a sensitive matter to speak about. The Pastor was very encouraging indeed because, quite unknown to me, the RAF Chaplain who originally invited me to be a Scripture Reader had sent a letter to the Pastor commending my action.

CHAPTER 16

There were a few patrols that the squadron had to make at the beginning of September, when we heard of the amphibious landings that had taken place on the Italian mainland. Mussolini had resigned back in May, so the new government immediately called for an armistice. The Italians were shown that their Axis alliance with Hitler was a mistake and we hoped that once surrender terms could be agreed, they would change sides and fight for us.

During the month one could sense that autumn was approaching, as the weather began to get colder and the days became noticeably shorter. I wondered what Ruth and the family might take to the Harvest Thanksgiving service on 26th September. Perhaps she would use a couple of the Wing Commander's apples to make some small apple pies, whilst my father would probably take a few of his potatoes. She told me that every day was so noisy, with troops being transported, operational exercises by the Home Guard, who had set up a small firing range in the near distance, or the drone of bombers going out on raids towards Germany or returning from their missions. This was quite stressful.

Although the Luftwaffe were now on the back foot now, they were very persistent with their bombing raids. They just would not accept that they were being beaten. At the beginning of October, with a cold wind in the air, we were scrambled to intercept a heavy raid on London. This time their fighter escort was minimal, so most of our pilots were able to make attacks on the enemy bombers, some of which included upgrades to the Junkers Ju88s, which appeared to be using new direction-finding equipment mounted and visible on their aircraft.

I was pulling out of a dive on my first attack when I heard "Blue Leader, there's a Dornier above you! Watch out for the tracer!" I looked over my shoulder to see the familiar wisps of red light drifting through the air, and they were getting closer. I felt a few bumps on the fuselage as I started weaving, then put the Spitfire on full throttle and went into a tight turn to starboard. This must have distracted the gunner, who still seemed to be aiming ahead of me on my original course. But my blood was up, and I wasn't going to let him go now. I brought my aircraft round, gaining height all the time, so by the time I'd come round in a full circle the

Dornier was just below and ahead of me, just where I wanted it. I cut the throttle slightly as I approached and pressed the gun button, and the cannon and machine-guns in the Spitfire's wings burst into life, throwing out a hail of deadly bullets towards my target. This time I was the one who wasn't going to miss.

As I watched, bits started flying off the Dornier's fuselage and engines, the undercarriage slowly lowered from under the engine nacelles, and the crew began to bale out. Another one up for me! When I got back, the fuselage of my plane had rather more holes in it than I would have liked, and one area of panelling looked like the top of a pepperpot.

The ground crew informed me that it would take a while to either repair or replace the damaged panels on my Spitfire, but this gave me a good chance to do more work as a Scripture Reader. I had spent much time talking to the pilots, helping them wherever I could, and trying to encourage them openly to give their lives to Christ. Unfortunately I had been so busy thinking about the constant enemy raids, and about my family as well, that I had to pray for forgiveness in putting these before God. It was a time when I really needed a sign as to how I was to proceed. Once again, God answered my prayer, because one of the rooms formerly used as a recreation hut by one of the other squadrons suddenly became vacant. It was said that they had begun to use the nearby school gymnasium, which was of a more modern design.

Again I asked the Wing Commander if we could use this for our regular prayer meetings and Bible studies. I explained my reasons for making this request. The Chaplain on the base knew of my standing as a Scripture Reader, and offered his support, but he added that I shouldn't be ashamed in any way, because there were always times when works like mine were hard to perform, simply because of the circumstances. We were fortunate in that the hut already contained a small number of chairs stacked up near the walls, and these we could move and use ourselves. The space was enough for us to hold a small service or meeting in, but there was already a nearby chapel where pilots attended services. However, we considered adding a small temporary partition to the hut to create a small office next to our new meeting room. This was done with the help of a local builder. It wasn't for a while that I worked out what we might use to play any hymns or choruses, but one of the pilots approached me with his accordion, and offered to act as a musician. Now we were really moving! By the end of October the Chaplain and I had arranged a schedule to start our Gospel work.

Wednesday 3rd November was a lovely sunny day. In the evening some of the pilots gathered in the meeting room, or Rest Room as it was now described, to listen to the Chaplain introduce me as a Scripture Reader in this new Bible study meeting. Most of them already knew of my deep Christian beliefs and had been grateful for the understanding word I had given them in their times of need, while some were men who may have been churchgoers in their childhood, but had either not continued as such, or possibly had turned away because the old traditional style of long sermon meant nothing to them.

As this was the first meeting, I started by reading a short, yet very important text: "For God so loved the world that he gave his only begotten Son, that whosoever believeth in him should not perish, but have everlasting life," (John 3:16) I told them that these words were the basis of the Gospel message, that Jesus came to save us from the power of sin and of the world. When he returns in glory, as is prophesied, there will only be one consequence for those who reject or deny him, and that is a fatal judgement by God. As humans we go through a life cycle, in that we are born, we live our lives through, and we die. Yet God offers us a new beginning in a life that is everlasting – God's eternal life.

A number showed interest, and commented that they had heard the text, but it had never been explained to them quite so fully. When they had attended their church in Canada, everyone seemed to believe that if they were churchgoers, they would go to heaven anyway. At this I warned them that if they had never made a personal commitment to believe in Jesus Christ, then they were denying him, and the result would be fatal.

Through November, word of my Bible meetings every Wednesday afternoon quickly spread around the base, and it wasn't long before both pilots and ground crew from the other squadrons started drifting in. It was a real blessing to know that there were pilots wanting to be converted. As they described it, it was better to be right with God today if one is going to die tomorrow at the hands of the Luftwaffe. Sadly, this was an event that still occurred regularly when intense raids were carried out.

Meanwhile, I was on really good terms with the Canadians on my squadron, and my French language skills were progressing steadily. There was one occasion of some amusement when I walked into the canteen and heard the words, "No bad language now, here comes the Preacher!" We all joined in the laughter but, as a measure of compromise, I told them of my story at the OTU where I had been nicknamed John the Baptist. I was told that during the Battle of Britain there were aces like Wing Commander Douglas Bader and Wing Commander J.E. "Johnnie" Johnson who had had their initials painted on their aircraft. They now had their own ace to identify, and when I walked out to my Spitfire the next morning I found that my original squadron ID and aircraft call-sign had been replaced by the letters 'J' and 'B', one on each side of the large RAF roundel on the fuselage. Douglas Bader's call-sign was 'Dogsbody', so I would become 'John-Boy'.

In December I was granted leave to go home for Mary's birthday. The Wing Commander's wife had knitted her a lovely pink cardigan, which made her feel quite special.

Ruth wrote to me the following week, telling me that Mary had only just discovered that I had also brought one for Ruby. With Christmas approaching, even though the Luftwaffe raids appeared to have reduced and the war in the Atlantic was being won, supplies were still short, and there were new restrictions on transport and furniture. Everything possible was being salvaged, whether it was car spares or the wool from old socks, and regular collections were made. Aluminium was one of the primary items that the government was looking for, because it all went toward the construction of new Spitfires.

CHAPTER 17

1944 began well for the Allies. Although the weather in Italy was really bad and the troops had to endure heavy rain, which subsequently delayed the advance because of the muddy roads the rain created, they now began to move northwards more steadily, if a little slowly. Mussolini had been ousted from power, and the new Italian government had already negotiated terms for an armistice. It appeared that most Italians had lost faith in 'Il Duce', as Mussolini had been nicknamed, and the war was bringing such hardship upon the population that they just wanted to end it, regardless of the cost.

The official Italian surrender had been signed in September 1943, but German forces had occupied two strong defensive lines in the north of the country, and

Mussolini himself, who had been released from prison by German paratroops, had established his own fascist government in the north. He took severe measures against many of those he saw as defeatist traitors, one of whom was his son-in-law Count Ciano, whom the Germans executed by firing squad after a drumhead trial.

A couple of months later, in March 1944, John's letters home suddenly stopped. Ruth was quite concerned, because her mind was still trying to work out what was happening. Shortly afterwards she received a black-bordered letter from the War Office, and read it with mounting horror. It stated: "We regret to inform you that your husband Flight Lieutenant John Wilkins has been posted as missing, presumed lost, on a mission over France." Ruth was devastated, but she was not one to give up hope easily. Even though he was missing, John could still be alive somewhere in France.

A week later Ruth received a personal message from John's Squadron Leader, telling them what had happened. He wrote "That day we had been ordered to join other squadrons on a special daylight mission into France, which in itself was unusual. You will appreciate that I cannot say what it was or where we went, due to secrecy. We were told that this was an important mission that required every available aircraft. We had suffered losses due to enemy attacks so, knowing of John's ability as a fighter pilot, I asked whether he would make up the necessary numbers on the squadron. He agreed, and took control of 'B' Flight in an older Spitfire Mark 5 that had only just been serviced, but not yet fully flight tested.

"When we took off from base John sent a radio message saying that the rudder on his aircraft felt a little sticky, but he felt he could manage it. As we crossed the French coast we must have been detected by enemy radar, because soon after that we were intercepted by a large number of enemy fighters, some of which were the new Focke-Wulf Fw190 fighters, which greatly outpaced us as they dived. In the dogfight that followed I saw John's wingman under attack. Without thinking of his own safety, John broke left and came in behind the Fw190, which had already scored several hits on his wingman. We believe the enemy pilot was concentrating so hard on getting a kill that he failed to look in his rear-view mirror, because John was able to get to close range before firing. We saw the fighter go down in flames, but John was then attacked by two more. This time he didn't make it. The last we saw was his plane trailing smoke and going down into the clouds in a spin. We've heard nothing from the enemy about his capture, so at present I can only assume the worst. John was a pillar of strength in this squadron. Not only was he an exceptional pilot, but the Christian faith and understanding that he demonstrated helped many men during the conflict. He was highly respected."

When Ruth showed John's father Charles the letter, he

wasn't too sure that all hope was lost. One of the first manoeuvres he had learned in the Tiger Moth was how to get out of a spin. It was dangerous, but it was certainly possible. Besides, there were areas of France that were quite hilly, and so were less well populated by both the Germans and the French. Charles was sure that once John had disappeared into the clouds then the enemy fighters would not follow him. In some ways, it was just like the memory of what had happened to him in the Great War.

At the beginning of April the old Pastor addressed the congregation during the Sunday service. He spoke of how John had come to serve God through his work in the church, and quoted the Scripture text: "Not slothful in business; fervent in spirit; serving the Lord. Rejoicing in hope; patient in tribulation, continuing instant in prayer." (Romans 12:11-12) The congregation then came together to pray for John, whatever his circumstances might be. Ruth still believed that her John could still return safely, even though there were no signs yet that he had survived. Whatever had happened, John would have wanted her to have faith in him.

Two months later, on 6th June 1944, the long awaited amphibious invasion of France took place. After a big coastal bombardment by the main fleet warships in the task force, made up of nearly 6,000 ships, thousands of British, American, Canadian, French and Colonial troops poured ashore in Normandy on D-Day. The British and Canadian beaches, named Gold, Juno and Sword, were taken with only moderate resistance. However, the Americans suffered heavy casualties on the two beaches named Omaha and Utah. On Omaha in particular the troops were landed some distance from the beach, and were mown down by heavy machine gun fire from expert troops manning the defences ahead of and on the high beach wall. No tank support was available, because the amphibious tanks or DUKWs were also deployed too far out from the beach and were simply swamped by the heavy waves. It was even thought at one point that the troops might have to withdraw, which had been the German Field Marshal Rommel's hope, but later in the day American engineers managed to blow a massive hole in the beach wall using Bangalore torpedoes, and the infantry started to swarm through the breach. Eventually the five beachheads linked up, and the liberation of France began.

Ruth had still had no reports about John, yet she remained confident in him. At home they cleaned his bedroom every week in preparation for the day he would return, although she did not know when that might be. It was as if time had simply stood still when John had returned to base, and absolutely nothing would be changed. Everything was in its rightful place, just where he had left it. It hurt Ruth to think she might not see John again, but she did not believe this would happen. All the time she had the support of Charles, who still declared his faith in John's flying ability, and the comfort she received from Alice, who still lived at home with her, and John's mother Maria.

As Allied troops advanced toward the German border later in the year, they suffered two big setbacks. The British Field Marshal Montgomery organized the drop of paratroopers in a mission to secure bridges across the main rivers in Holland. He had hoped that once this was done then a tank force could advance promptly, secure the bridges and create a gap in the German defences through which other units could advance. It was not known that German Intelligence already knew of the plan, named Operation Market Garden. When the paratroopers were dropped they found reinforcements of fanatical and merciless SS troops who had been re-equipping near the drop zone at Arnhem. Although the British Parachute force managed to repulse the first enemy counter-attacks, they found that their radio sets weren't working properly. It was only a matter of time before they would be overcome. Eventually the soldiers who had survived the assault were given orders to withdraw back across the river in whatever way they could.

The Allies were still hoping for a prompt end to the war, perhaps even by Christmas, but they were in for a shock. On 16th December 1944 Hitler took a last gamble and ordered a massive assault by large numbers of troops, supported by tanks, including the latest Tigers, through the wooded region of the Ardennes. They were to head on a narrow front towards the Dutch city of Antwerp, which had a deep harbour that the Allies relied upon for supplies. The

Germans knew that there were only a limited number of American troops guarding the Ardennes region, many of whom had little or no combat experience, simply because the Americans did not believe that such a heavily-wooded area could be penetrated by tanks. The main problem for the Germans was the lack of fuel for the vehicles taking part in the attack, particularly the tanks. They hoped to capture American fuel depots on the way.

At first the attack went well, and German troops in white winter clothing started to advance with tank support towards the town of Bastogne, an important town covering the junction between seven main roads. If they captured Bastogne, they would control the roads. Only a desperate defence by men who included troops from the famed 101st Airborne 'Screaming Eagles' prevented the occupation of the town. Although the enemy had created a big bulge in the Allied lines, they had not captured any fuel dumps. The foggy weather was clearing, which allowed Allied aircraft to take off and attack tanks, which were simply running out of fuel, and any other enemy troops or vehicles that they saw. By the middle of January, nearly a month after the first assault, the Battle of the Bulge, as it came to be known, was over.

For Ruth in particular, the month of December 1944 was one of turmoil. Little Mary celebrated her seventh birthday on the 8th December. It was only the second time John had missed being at home with Mary for her birthday, and Ruth heard her little voice saying "Where's Daddy? Will he be here soon?", a question that Ruth simply couldn't answer. She tried telling Mary that her Daddy was a soldier who was fighting against all the bad things in the world, and that sometimes soldiers had to go and fight when and where their officers ordered them to go, and the soldiers, even though they were brave, couldn't always do what they wanted, or go where they wanted. Ruth certainly didn't want to say that Mary might never see her father again.

She celebrated Christmas with Mary, Alice, Charles, Maria, and Ruby as well, but the festivities were muted. Even the King's speech offered little consolation or comfort. He spoke of the need to create a world of free men, untouched by tyranny, then continued "I wish you, from my heart, a happy Christmas, and, for the coming year, a full measure of courage and faith in God which alone enables us to bear old sorrows and face new trials, until the day when the Christmas message – peace on earth and goodwill towards men – finally comes true." But to Ruth there could be no peace in her heart unless John was there to share it, or at least if she knew what had happened to him. She felt tormented by unbelievers who claimed that there was no reason to believe that John ever would return. She missed him so much, and there were constant tears in her eyes, but her prayers for him continued. At first she had prayed simply for his safety, but in view of what everyone had been saying, she added a little more to her faithful prayer. She said that, when Jesus was on this earth, one of the miracles He had performed was to bring Lazarus back from the dead. If God could do such wonders then, could he not do it now? After all, John had been a faithful servant to him.

Ruth still kept her memories of John close to her heart, even though she had heard nothing for nine months. Because she was still young, and a single mother, questions were even asked here and there as to how long she could go on like that. Yet three months later Ruth was to find a new joy that would change her life again.

CHAPTER 18

Three months after Christmas, at the end of March 1945, Ruth was at home with Alice and little Mary when they suddenly saw a man in a long blue trench coat and carrying a large kitbag open the gate at the bottom of their garden and slowly tread up the path to the front door. The man's face was bearded, weather-beaten and worn, but she recognized him right away. It was John!

Ruth rushed out of the door, ran down the path and gazed at him in wonder before they fell into each other's arms. His eyes were tired, but his face showed his sense of peace, relief and joy at being back home. As they walked through the door, together once again, little Mary saw him too. She jumped down happily off her chair with open arms, shouting excitedly "Daddy! Daddy!" It was as if he'd never left. John picked her up, perhaps a little wearily, and remarked how much she had grown since he'd been away.

Right away Ruth called Charles and Maria on the phone to tell them that John had returned. She could guess from his response that he was smiling to himself and thinking "I knew he'd make it back!" John told Ruth that he had been given two weeks' leave on medical grounds, but he needed a couple of days to rest before he would feel ready to tell his story.

So it was that a couple of days later, on the last day of March, the family came together to hear what had happened. First of all, John told them that the squadron had been on a high-level mission over a rather remote area of north-east France when they had been intercepted by enemy fighters, including a number of the latest Focke-Wulf Fw190 fighters. As a big dogfight broke out, they dropped their long-range fuel tanks, but John had seen his wingman in trouble and moved across to protect him, which he did with great success. Unfortunately his rudder controls weren't operating correctly, so when he was attacked by other enemy fighters, he found that he couldn't turn inside them. They were able to concentrate fire on him for a few seconds and, though he was unhurt, they damaged the engine and fuselage on his Spitfire. Spitfires could take a lot of damage, but probably not as much as the fabric-covered fuselage of the Hurricane, and the engine was the heart of it all. Once that went, the plane was dead. The glycol coolant was already alight and pouring out of the exhausts on the cowling, which caused him to trail a great deal of smoke. The engine was running roughly, and because the controls weren't operating correctly he only had one option, which was to dive for the clouds to try and escape. His radio had also been shot up, so there was no way he could communicate.

Even before he had reached cloud cover the Spitfire had turned over and gone into a spin, and he had no chance of baling out anyway because the cockpit cover had jammed. The only way he could go was down. Because of the thick cloud cover the enemy fighters must have turned away, leaving him as a 'probable' victim rather than claiming a confirmed kill.

His plane was accelerating, but he remembered what Charles and his advanced flying instructor had said about getting out of a spin, which was to try and turn into it. He had succeeded in pulling out of a spin in the much slower Tiger Moth, but at first he wasn't sure whether the accelerating Spitfire would make it. At less than 2,000 feet he managed to regain some sort of control over the plane, though he knew it was too badly damaged to try and get back to base. If he lost any more height it would be too low for him to bale out anyway, even if he could free the jammed cockpit cover. He had been flying over one of the hillier regions of France, and was looking desperately for a field where he could land.

By this time the undercarriage lever wasn't even working, so it had to be a belly-landing. A mile or two ahead he saw a small area of grassland, for which he headed. It was only just in time, because the engine was coughing badly by now, and wouldn't last long. He tried to put the flaps down, but they were only partially operative. John also knew that if he simply cut the throttle drastically he might simply nose-dive into the ground, so it had to be very gradual. By the time he reached the grassy area his airspeed was about right, so he brought the Spitfire in slowly, not knowing whether it might explode on landing. By this time searing fumes were coming in through the floor of the cockpit, and he could feel the pain as they started to burn through his flying gear. As he pancaked the Spitfire it almost bounced, but the tail lifted and the propeller blades dug into the ground as the plane came to a halt.

He was lucky; it didn't explode. But this wasn't the time to think about how good a landing he'd made. As he smashed the Perspex cockpit cover to escape he realized that the enemy must have seen his plane in trouble and were probably heading for it in half-tracks right now. If the aircraft was left as it was and they couldn't find the pilot's body, they would immediately assume he had escaped and hunt him down. John was going to try and deceive them. The damage on the wings had already caused the self-sealing fuel tanks to rupture, and he could see the fuel already dripping down. There was also oil dripping from the tanks in the wing. Because of this he grabbed the water bottle that many pilots took with them, emptied it, and refilled it with some of the dripping fuel. He then took out his handkerchief and twisted it into the neck of the bottle. Once that was complete he lit the end of the handkerchief, tossed the bottle into the cockpit, and ran for cover. A few moments later there was a massive explosion in the cockpit, followed by other explosions as both fuel and ammunition went up. John smiled to himself. The enemy certainly wouldn't find anything now.

He slowly made his way towards a village which from his pocket map appeared to be called Sauveur-sous-Mont, literally 'Rescuer under the hill'. It was an unusual name, but one that seemed quite appropriate under the circumstances. In the distance he could see a large building, but at first, he couldn't see what it was. As he drew closer the burning in his legs started to slow him down, but he suddenly made out some people outside the gates wearing black gowns and white headpieces. It must be a convent.

He was only a few hundred yards away when the nuns saw him and approached him. He was feeling the pain in his legs so much that he simply collapsed unconscious on the ground. When he came to he found himself in what appeared to be a giant wine cellar, being tended by two of the nuns. A short time later the Mother Superior approached him and said that they had treated his wounds. John was thankful, yet alarmed, because the Germans had always threatened to execute any of the French whom they found collaborating with the enemy. The Mother Superior smiled and said that even though the Germans occasionally searched the convent, it was quite a random affair, and the soldiers always cut their search short if they were provided with a couple of bottles of wine from the convent's own vineyard nearby. He would be in no danger. She also explained the unusual name of the village. She said that many years before the houses in the village had been far more scattered, and during the winter the two nearby mountains were always thick with snow and ice. There had been massive snowfalls, and the only building strong enough to resist the snowfalls was the sturdy convent. Many had sheltered there, and if their own homes were destroyed, they were rebuilt in the vicinity of the convent. The convent had been a rescuer, hence the name of the village.

CHAPTER 19

It took several weeks for John to recover from his injuries, but the convent remained undisturbed by any German patrols. In mid-April the Priest at the nearby Catholic Church, Father Pierre, came to see him, and declared that it would be very difficult for him to make his way back to England. The local Resistance group could probably give him some help, but it might take several months before they could work anything out. He said that there were new rumours of a forthcoming Allied invasion, and the Germans were busy strengthening their defences. Had John himself got any ideas?

There was certainly one possibility. Rather than make a dangerous attempt to escape, which stood little or no chance of success, could he not elude the enemy by disguising himself? During his time at Carlington Bible College John had studied the Roman Catholic Church, and how it worked. Because of his time as a Pastor, and as a Scripture Reader in the RAF, his experience of giving sermons, and with his fairly good knowledge of the French language, could he not temporarily disguise himself as a Catholic priest? If Father Pierre could provide him with a gown and offer him some guidance along the way, whilst the Resistance provided him with false identity papers, he would be able to work at the church without the slightest suspicion from the enemy. It seemed a wild notion to start with, but the Father thought it was so original that it might just work. If the liberation of France was also on the cards, then John might just keep everything going until Allied forces arrived.

The leader of the Resistance group thought everything sounded too easy. If the Germans had a plant or collaborator in the church, of all places, they would quickly hear who was who in the area.

The following day two men from the Resistance grabbed John from the convent, blindfolded and gagged him, then led him on an arduous uphill trek into one of the thickly-wooded areas on the mountain. When the blindfold was removed he found himself standing before a burly, roughly-dressed group of men armed with an assortment of weapons, from captured machine-guns to pistols. He felt like the Sheriff of Nottingham standing in front of Robin Hood and his band of outlaws. John had a good idea of French conversation from his classes at the Squadron Base, so when the bearded man who appeared to be the leader of the group suddenly addressed him, he was able to respond in French. He was asked the usual questions, name, rank and number, and then what his squadron was, and what aircraft he flew. John replied that he couldn't answer that because of secrecy, but the leader started shouting at him, saying that John was a plant. He claimed that the real pilot was dead, and that John was just acting out a good role so he could spy for the Germans.

John tried to stay calm, but in the face of all the danger before him he wasn't quite sure how he could convince the men of the Resistance, and their leader in particular, of his true identity. However, he lost his cool for once when the leader came up to him and slapped him suddenly twice across the face. What he said was not exemplary of an English priest, but the leader then turned to him and apologised with a smile, saying that they had to make sure about him first. They agreed to provide false identity papers, and after a celebratory cup of coffee with the men John stood with his cup in the air in front of them and declared "Vive la France!", to which they responded with a loud cheer. John felt that he had made his mark amongst the men, and they had accepted him favourably.

Two weeks later Father Pierre arrived at the convent with a small package. He had done as John had suggested and brought his spare priest's gown for him to try on for size.

The two men were quite similar in size, so the gown fitted very comfortably. He then reached into his pocket and took out some identity papers, on which the photo showed him with the beard he had already grown. He looked quite indistinguishable from the RAF fighter pilot who had begun the mission. He told John that the new papers would identify him as Brother Jean, a Transitional Deacon from Boulogne who had recently joined the church and been sent for practical experience to the church at Sauveur-sous-Mont. He also promised to take him to the church and remind him of some of the duties that a Catholic priest might need to perform. This included some of the particular ways in which a Catholic service was conducted. He would also need to know the name of the senior priest through whom the appointment was made, but Father Pierre declared that there was nothing to worry about, because he had some good friends in high places in the church. The practical experience that John gained over the next few weeks under the guidance of Father Pierre was invaluable. John, now known as Brother Jean, soon moved into the home next to the Catholic Church, where Father Pierre had arranged accommodation for him.

At the service John attended with Father Pierre, he was surprised to see a few German soldiers amongst the congregation. The Father introduced him as a new priest who had been invited to join them, then invited John to read the Scripture text for the day, which he did very competently. It was to be an introduction to his new life for several months to come. He remarked that as those months went by the soldiers became more and more nervous as the tide of the war turned against them. They heard of the D-Day landings on 6th June 1944, then another amphibious landing in the south of France in August. Disillusioned officers even tried to assassinate Hitler on 20th July, an act which incurred Hitler's wrath and caused the death of a number of senior officers whom he believed to be involved in the plot against him, including Field Marshal Rommel. As the Allied forces advanced through France, and Russian forces kept up the pressure in the east, any number of Germans could have believed that the war was already lost. They wanted to survive, just like the French villagers, but they were still soldiers under orders, so they had to be treated with great caution.

Over the Christmas period the German Army broke through the American lines and advanced considerably during the Battle of the Bulge, but that moment of encouragement disappeared when the Americans counter-attacked and forced the enemy to retreat right back to their starting point. Then one could see their feelings change to real fear, for they heard that not only were the Allied forces advancing once again in the west but according to some reports, they were only a few miles from the village. The Russians had also begun a big move in the east. Would they be cut off?

John was able to talk to some of the soldiers, who now believed that the war was lost and that Hitler had caused all their problems. What could they do? He told them a worldly army could be defeated, but that all who joined the army of Christ would be victorious in the end. There were many to whom patriotism meant all, and even in the face of defeat they stood their ground. Unfortunately the Resistance, now well armed, got to them first. Only one man, having seen the error and futility of his ways, discarded his uniform and came to Father Pierre for help. When the Allies liberated the town the soldier wanted to don his uniform once again and surrender, though John went with him to the army base to ensure he received fair treatment, something which John believed the soldier appreciated.

However, there was an even bigger surprise to come. Whilst they were in the Colonel's office at the army base John revealed his true identity, removing the priest's gown to reveal his RAF uniform, which was still smart, if a little worn. He said afterwards that had never seen so many people's jaws drop in his life. They were quite astounded at his story, but they made official enquiries with the RAF to confirm John's identity, and accepted that he was who he said he was.

Because of what John had achieved, the Colonel himself made a point of booking him a place on one of the next C47 transports that were taking some of the wounded home.

When he got back it was as if the landscape had been completely redesigned, full of as many American soldiers as British, and an air of eagerness to end the war in Europe which, everyone agreed, could only go on for a few weeks more.

CHAPTER 20

Once home, John started to grow stronger in both mind and body and soon started to make and renew friendships, both in the village and further afield. Rather than be posted for combat duties, he was used by the RAF in a few cases as something of a morale-booster or propaganda machine, which he hated. He would stand on a stage in a particular town or city and give his story to the seated crowd. Although the death of the American President, Franklin D. Roosevelt, cast a cloud over the expected celebrations, nothing could stop the feeling that the war would soon be over.

Once the European War was over and the war in Asia was in its final stages, John accepted the fact that his time in the RAF was over. John, Ruth and Mary had spent so much time apart that over the next few months there was a great deal of catching up to do. The world had changed, and even though they spent many happy times together, there was much to be done at home.

Many of the tutors at Carlington Bible College were still working there, and one had become the Principal since the Reverend Greenaway had passed away peacefully at the end of 1945. He was a man to be missed, yet remembered with admiration for the large part that he had played in our lives.

One of John's best friends, Jimmy Whiteside, had been released from the RAF and had become a policeman, where he felt he could put his disciplinary measures to good use. He also tracked down his former CO and flying instructor from the Training Unit, who was maintaining his skills as an instructor at a rural flying club. He wrote to Father Pierre, but it was over two months before he heard back. He was well, but he added that there had been a fire at the church after the liberation, so it would take much time and effort to repair it. Because of what Father Pierre had done for him through that fateful year of 1944, John decided to organize a collection that he could send as a small donation toward the repair of the church.

As for his other family and friends at home, Charles and Maria had endured the war under some hardship. Though the farm was doing well, the labour involved had taken its toll. Also, they had made sure that my family, and particularly the children, had enough to eat, even if they went a little short themselves. After all, one cannot exactly live on rabbit pie and nothing else. There was tragic news about Jacob, whose loyalty had meant so much to Charles. Jacob had been a co-pilot of an Avro Lancaster sent on a heavy raid to Berlin. Because Berlin was the capital of the German Reich it was heavily defended, and they found that Jacob was one of the unlucky ones who had been hit by the anti-aircraft fire. They were told by his family that the searchlights had suddenly locked onto his bomber, so that the guns were able to concentrate their fire upon him, and the Lancaster went down in flames over the target. There were no survivors.

Alice, who had always played an active role as a teacher, wanted to continue in this role. She declared that now the war was over children should be entitled to a good education, whatever the status of their parents. Ruby had truly become like little Mary's big sister, but there came a time when even she had to leave. Her parents had escaped the bombing in the central areas of Bristol and were getting their lives back together. One day they arrived in the village by car and asked where their daughter had been staying. After a while they arrived on John and Ruth's doorstep, and Ruby saw them immediately. They told of the damage that had been caused in Bristol because of the air raids, and said efforts were already being made to repair this, though it would take some time. Although there was a tinge of sadness in their voices when Ruby had to leave and rejoin her parents, she and Mary hugged each other and promised to keep in touch. Ruby's parents were grateful for the way they had looked after their little girl, and wondered if there was any way that they could repay them. John said that to have the satisfaction of knowing that their daughters had become almost inseparable friends was reward enough.

As for the smiling old Pastor, soon after the end of the war he at last accepted that his time in the job was done. He knew John had trusted him all the way through and was minded to return to a role in the church. For this reason he asked John to become the deputy Pastor once again during the short time he had left and then, on the Pastor's retirement, John would be officially inducted as the official Church Minister. The Pastor told him he had earned it.

There is so much more that could be told, but that remains to be written.

ACKNOWLEDGEMENTS

The Holy Bible (King James Version)

Sovereign Service, Colonel Ian Dobbie

A Very Present Help, Lieutenant General Sir William Dobbie

Fighting Aircraft of World War II, Bill Gunston

Christmas on the Home Front, Mike Brown

Handbook of World War II, Karen Farrington

ND - #0157 - 270225 - C0 - 203/127/12 - PB - 9781861517685 - Gloss Lamination